D0171192

DISCARD

"A Rich Husband Is All You Need To Keep The Baby?"

She nodded. "For my family to see me as the perfect mother?" She gave a fake trilling laugh. "Oh, yes, a husband is the must-have accessory of the season. The richer, the better."

His lips quirked in a smile, his eyes crinkling at the corners, just a hint of cockiness. The expression gave her pause, because he wasn't laughing at her joke. No, she knew this look, too. It was his *I've solved the problem* look. "I think we've got that covered."

"Excuse me?"

"You said it yourself. All you need is a rich, successful husband."

For a moment she just stared blankly at him, unable to follow the abrupt twist the conversation had taken. "Right. A rich, successful husband. Which I don't have."

"But you could." He smiled fully now. Full smiles were rare for him. Usually they made her feel a little breathless. This one just made her nervous. "All you have to do is marry me."

Dear Reader,

I worked really hard last year. I'm not complaining, mind you…just mentioning it. Here's one of the weird things about me: when I'm writing a book, I can't read anyone else's books. I need to be completely in my own story. So last year, when I was working hard, I didn't read much.

Oh, man, I missed it.

So, over Christmas, when I took a break, I read, read, read. Seven books and some 3,600 pages later, I finally feel like myself again. And I've decided I never again want to go so long without reading fiction.

So why am I sharing this with you? Shouldn't I instead be telling you all about the book you're about to read? (A sexy tycoon, a plucky heroine, an orphaned baby…there, now you know the highlights.) But I'm baring my soul about this because it just seems like you'll understand. After all, you're a reader, too. You know what joy it brings. You've felt the excitement that vibrates just beneath the surface of your day when you know you've got a great book waiting for you at home. I hope that this book brings you some small measure of the same pleasure that my holiday reading brought to me.

As always, thank you for letting me entertain you!

Emily McKay

The Tycoon's Temporary Baby

EMILY McKAY

All the characters in this book have no existence outside the imagination of the author, and have no relation whatsoever to anyone bearing the same name or names. They are not even distantly inspired by any individual known or unknown to the author, and all the incidents are pure invention.

First published in Great Britain 2012
by Mills & Boon, an imprint of Harlequin (UK) Limited.
Large Print edition 2012
Harlequin (UK) Limited,
Eton House, 18-24 Paradise Road,
Richmond, Surrey TW9 1SR

ISBN: 978 0 263 22965 3

Harlequin (UK) policy is to use papers that are natural, renewable and recyclable products and made from wood grown in sustainable forests. The logging and manufacturing process conform to the legal environmental regulations of the country of origin.

Printed and bound in Great Britain
by CPI Antony Rowe, Chippenham, Wiltshire

EMILY McKAY

has been reading romance novels since she was eleven years old. Her first Romance book came free. She has been reading and loving romance novels ever since. She lives in Texas with her geeky husband, her two kids and too many pets. Her debut novel, *Baby, Be Mine*, was a RITA® Award finalist for Best First Book and Best Short Contemporary. She was also a 2009 *RT Book Reviews* Career Achievement nominee for Series Romance. To learn more, visit her website at www.EmilyMcKay.com

For Tracy and Shellee,
two great friends and phenomenal writers. Ladies, thanks for making this so much fun. And to Ivy Adams, 'cause…well, you know.

One

Jonathon Bagdon just wanted his assistant to come home, damn it.

Wendy Leland had left seven days ago to attend a family funeral. In the time she'd been gone, his whole company had started falling apart. A major deal she'd been finessing had fallen through. He'd missed an important deadline because the first temp had erased his online calendar. The second temp had accidentally sent R&D's latest prototype to Beijing instead of Bangalore. The head of HR had threatened to quit twice. And no fewer than five women had run out of his office in tears.

As if all of that wasn't bad enough, the fourth temp had deep-fried the coffee maker. So he hadn't had a decent cup of coffee in three days. All in all, this was not his best moment.

Was it really too much to ask that at this particular time—when both of his business partners were out of town and when he was putting the finishing touches on the proposal for a crucial contract—that his assistant just come home?

Jonathon stared into his mug of instant coffee, contemplating whether he could ask Jeanell—the head of HR—to go out and buy a coffee maker, or if that would send her over the edge. Not that Jeanell was at the office yet. Most of the staff wandered in sometime around nine. It was barely seven.

Yes, he could have just gone out to buy himself a cup o' joe—or better yet, a new coffee maker—but with one deadline after another piling up, he just didn't have time for this crap. If Wendy had been here, a new coffee maker would have magically appeared. The same way the deal with Olson Inc. would have gone through without a hitch. When Wendy was here, things just worked. How was it that in the short five years she'd been the executive assistant here she'd become as crucial to the running of the company as he himself was?

Hell, if this past week was any indication, she was actually more important than he was. A sobering thought for a man who'd helped to build an empire out of nothing.

He knew only one thing, when Wendy did get back, he was going to do his damnedest to make sure she never left again.

Wendy Leland crept into the executive office of FMJ headquarters a little after seven. The motion sensor brought the lights up as she entered and she reached down to extend the canopy on the infant car seat she carried. Peyton, the tiny baby inside, frowned but remained asleep. She made a soft gurgling sound as Wendy lowered the car seat to a darkened corner behind her desk.

She rocked the seat gently until Peyton stilled, then Wendy dropped into her own swivel chair. Swallowing past the knot of dread in her throat, Wendy studied the office.

For five years, this had been the seat from which she'd surveyed her domain. She'd served as executive assistant for the three men who ran FMJ: Ford Langley, Matt Ballard and Jonathon Bagdon.

Her five years of Ivy League education made her perhaps a tad over-educated for the job. Or maybe not, since she hadn't procured an actual degree in any of her seven majors. Her family still thought she was wasting her talents. But the work was challenging and varied. She'd loved every minute of it. Nothing could have convinced her to leave FMJ.

Nothing, except the little bundle of joy asleep in the car seat.

When she'd left Palo Alto for Texas to attend her cousin Bitsy's funeral, she'd had no idea what awaited her. From the moment her mother called her to tell her that Bitsy had died in a motorcycle crash, the week had been one shock after another. She hadn't even known that Bitsy had a child. No one in the family had. Yet, now here Wendy was, guardian to an orphaned four-month-old baby. And gearing up for a custody battle of epic proportions. Peyton Morgan might as well have been dipped in gold the way the family was fighting over her. If Wendy wanted any chance of winning, she'd have to do the one thing she'd sworn she'd never do: move back to Texas. And that meant resigning from FMJ.

Only Bitsy could create this many problems from the grave.

Wendy gave a snort of laughter at the thought. Grief welled up in the wake of the humor. Squeezing her eyes shut, she pressed the heels of her hands against her eye sockets. Exhaustion had made her punchy, and if she gave in to her sorrow now, she might not stop crying for a month.

There would be time to grieve later. Right now, she had other things to take care of.

Wendy flicked on the desktop computer. Last night, she'd drafted the letter of resignation and then emailed it to herself. Of course, she could have sent it straight to Ford, Matt and Jonathon. She'd even spoken to Ford last night on the phone when he called to offer his condolences. Physically handing in the letter was a formality, but she wanted the closure that would come with printing it out, signing it and hand delivering it to Jonathon.

She owed him—or rather FMJ—that much at least. Before her life became chaotic, she wanted to take this one moment to say goodbye to the Wendy she had been and to the life she'd lived in Palo Alto.

Beside her, the computer hummed to life with a familiarity that soothed her nerves. A few clicks later, she'd opened the letter and routed it to the printer. The buzz of the printer seemed to echo through the otherwise quiet office. No one else was here this early. No one but Jonathon, who worked a grueling schedule.

After signing the letter, she left it on her desk and crossed to the closed door that separated her office from theirs. A wave of regret washed over her. She pressed her palm flat to the door, and then with a sigh, dropped her forehead onto the wood just above her hand. The door was solid beneath her head. Sturdy. Dependable. And she felt herself leaning against it, needing all the strength she could borrow.

"You can hardly blame Wendy," Matt Ballard pointed out, a note of censure in his voice. At the moment, Matt was in the Caribbean, on his honeymoon. It was why they'd scheduled this conference call for so early. Matt's new wife, Claire, allowed him exactly one business call a day. "It's the first time in five years she's taken personal leave."

"I didn't say I blamed her—" Jonathon said into the phone, now sorry he'd called Matt at all. He'd had a legitimate reason for calling, but now it sounded as though he was just whining.

"When is she supposed to be back?" Matt asked.

"She was supposed to be back four days ago." She'd said she'd be in Texas two to three days, tops. After the funeral, she'd called from Texas to say she'd have to stay "a little longer." The lack of specificity made him nervous.

"Stop worrying," Matt told him. "We'll have

plenty of time after Ford and I get back." As if it wasn't bad enough that Matt was on his honeymoon during this crisis, Ford and his family were also away, at their second home in New York City. "The proposal isn't due for nearly a month."

Yes. That was what bothered him. "Nearly a month" and "plenty of time" were about as imprecise as "a little longer." Jonathon was a man who liked precise numbers. If he was putting together an offer for a company worth millions, it mattered if the company was worth ten million or a hundred million. And even if he had nearly a month to work on the proposal, he wanted to know how long a little longer was.

Rather than take out his frustrations on his partner, Jonathon ended the phone call. This government contract was driving him crazy. Worse still was the fact that no one else seemed to be worried about it. For the past several years, research and development at FMJ had been perfecting smart grid meters, devices that could monitor and regulate a building's energy use. FMJ's system was more efficient and better designed than anything else on the market. Since they'd been using them at headquarters, they'd cut their electricity bills by thirty percent. This government contract would put FMJ's smart grid meters in every federal building in the country. The private sector would follow. Plus the meters would boost sales of other FMJ products. How could he not be excited about something that was going to cut energy consumption and make FMJ so much money?

Everything he'd been working for and planning for the past decade hinged on this one deal. It was the stepping-stone to FMJ's future. But first they had to actually get the contract.

Once he snapped his laptop closed, he heard a faint thump at the door. He wasn't optimistic enough to imagine the temp might come in this early. But did he even dare hope that Wendy had finally returned?

He pushed back his chair and strode across the oversize office he normally shared with Matt and Ford. When he opened the door, Wendy fell right into his arms.

Though unexpectedly falling through an open door seemed an apt metaphor for her life at the moment, nevertheless Wendy was surprised to find herself actually falling through the doorway. Jonathon's arms instantly wrapped around her, cradling her safely against his strong chest. One shoulder was pressed against him and her free hand automatically came up to the lapel of his suit jacket.

Suddenly she was aware of several things. The sharply crisp scent of his soap. The sheer breadth of his chest. And the clean, just-shaven line of his jaw, which was the first thing she saw when she looked up.

Normally, she did a decent job of ignoring it, but Jonathon Bagdon was the stuff of pure, girlish fantasies. He always looked on the verge of frowning, which lent his expression an air of thoughtful intensity. Though he rarely smiled, when he did, deep dimples creased his cheeks.

At just shy of six feet, he wasn't too tall, but his physique more than made up for what he lacked in height. He had a build more suited to barroom brawls than boardroom negotiations. He was strong and muscular. She'd never seen his naked chest, but he had a habit of shucking his suit jacket and rolling up the sleeves of his white dress shirt when he worked. Obviously she spent too much time looking at him. But until this moment, she'd never noticed he had a single mole on the underside of his perfectly square jaw.

Staring up into his green-brown eyes, she felt something unexpected pass between them. An awareness maybe. Some tension she'd never felt before. Or perhaps something she was too smart to let herself feel.

He swallowed. Fascinated, she watched the muscles of his throat shift mere inches from her face. She flattened her palm and pushed herself out of his arms.

She was all too aware of Jonathon's gaze following her every move. And even more aware that her outfit was inappropriate for work. He'd never seen her in jeans before. Certainly not topped with her favorite T-shirt, a retro Replacements concert T-shirt she'd bought online as her twenty-first birthday present to herself. It was old and ratty and she'd cut the neck out of it years ago. But somehow the shirt was all comfort. And today, she needed comfort more than she needed professionalism.

But, dang it, she wished he would stop looking at her with that hungry look.

It wasn't the first time in the five years they'd worked together that she'd seen him look at her like that. As if she was a temptation he had to resist. But it was the first time she'd allowed herself to feel even the faintest bit of need in return. Jonathon may be the stuff of feminine fantasies, but he was hell on women. She'd watched up close and personal as he'd trampled countless female hearts. She'd promised herself long ago that she'd never join the legions of women crushed by Jonathon Bagdon.

She could only hope that this new awareness she felt for him was the result of her exhaustion. Or perhaps her emotional vulnerability. Or maybe some bizarre hormone malfunction. At any rate, she wouldn't be around long enough for it to matter.

Jonathon wanted to pull her back into his arms. He didn't, of course. But he wanted to.

Instead, he held open the office door with one hand and shoved the other deep into his pants pocket, hoping to hide the effect her nearness had had on his body. As ridiculous as it was, in the few seconds he'd held his tempting little assistant against his chest, his body had responded. Only her shoulder and her palm had touched him and he'd still gone rock hard.

Of course, he'd felt that punch of desire for Wendy before. But normally he was better at schooling his response to her. Then again, she was usually dressed in blandly professional, business casual clothes. Not today. Her faded jeans were skintight and her T-shirt hung loose on her, its wide neck baring a tempting swath of collarbones, part of one shoulder and a hot pink bra strap.

He swallowed again, forcing his gaze back up to her face, searching for something to say. Something other than "Lose the shirt."

"I trust your trip went well," he finally ventured.

She frowned and took another step back.

Then he remembered she'd been to a funeral. Hardly the kind of trip that would go *well.* "I'm sorry for your loss," he added. Her frown deepened. Were those tears in her eyes? "However, I am very glad to have you back."

He sounded like an idiot. Which was not wholly unexpected. He didn't deal well with emotional women.

"I—" she started.

Then she broke off again. She turned away from him and pressed her hands to her face. If the tension in her shoulders was any indication, she was about two seconds away from bursting into tears.

In five years, Wendy had been nothing but completely professional. If she was going to break into tears, why couldn't she have done it when Ford was here to deal with her? Ford had three sisters, a mother, a stepmother, a wife and a daughter. Surely all of those women in his life had better prepared him for dealing with this sort of thing.

Jonathon followed her into the front office and

placed a hand on her back. He meant it to be comforting, but he was instantly aware that he'd placed it on the shoulder bared by her shirt. She twisted to look at him, her eyes wide and surprised, damp with unshed tears, but lit with something else as well. Beneath his hand her skin was hot, the strap of her bra silky and tempting.

She bit her lip again before pulling free of his touch.

And then he heard it. The unmistakable sound of crying. But not a woman crying. And it wasn't coming from Wendy.

Confused, he walked in and scanned the room for the source of the sound. It wasn't all-out screaming. More of a soft, mewling noise. Like a puppy might make. The room appeared empty. He moved toward the sound as Wendy rushed up behind him and practically threw herself in his path.

"I can explain!" She held up her hands in front of her as if warding off an attack.

"Explain what?" He dodged around her to look behind the desk. Her chair had been shifted to the side and where Wendy normally sat was an infant's car seat. And in that was a pale pink bundle.

He turned back to Wendy. "What is that?"

"That's a baby."

* * *

Jonathon's shock was palpable.

If she didn't know better, Wendy would have thought he'd never even seen a baby before. Though she imagined they were rare in his life, surely he had encountered at least one. After all, Ford had one himself. Jonathon must have been in the same room as his best friend's child at some point.

She dashed around him and squatted beside the car seat. She gave the back of it a gentle nudge but Peyton continued to fuss. Peyton's sleepy eyes flickered open, blinked and then focused on Wendy.

Something inside of Wendy tightened into a knot. A gut-level reaction to those bright blue eyes. Perhaps the only thing she'd ever felt that was actually stronger than that burst of attraction she'd felt for Jonathon just now.

Of course, she couldn't *have* Jonathon. She wasn't stupid enough to try. But for now, she did have Peyton. And she'd do anything in her power to keep her.

She unfastened the buckle strapping Peyton in and picked up the pink cotton bundle. Snuggling the baby close to her chest, she pressed her lips near Peyton's ear and made shushing noises. Then she drew in a breath scented like tear-free shampoo and pure love.

Suddenly feeling self-conscious, she looked up to find Jonathon watching her, a frown on his face.

She tried to smile but felt it wavering under the weight of her shifting emotions. "Jonathon, meet Peyton."

"Right," he said bracingly and he looked from her to the baby and then all around the room as if searching for the spaceship that must have dropped off this strange creature. "What is it doing in our office?"

"*She's* here because I brought her here." Which maybe hadn't been the smartest move, but she and Peyton had only gotten in the previous evening, after driving from Boulder, Colorado. With less than seventy-two hours of parenting experience under her belt, Wendy hadn't known what else to do with Peyton. "I didn't have anyone to watch her. And I don't think she's ready to be left with a stranger yet anyway. I mean, I'm strange enough, right? And—"

Jonathon cut her off. "Wendy, why do you have a baby?" His gaze dropped to her belly, suspicion lighting his gaze. "She's not…yours, is she?"

She was glad he'd cut her off, because she'd been babbling, but at the same time dreading the conversation to come, because he was not going to like what she had to say. Still, when she glanced down at the sixteen-pound baby, she had to laugh.

"No, I didn't go away for seven days and miraculously get pregnant, gestate and deliver a four-month-old. She's—" Her throat closed over the words, but she forced herself to say them. "She was my cousin's. Bitsy named me guardian. So she is mine now."

There was a long moment of silence during which Jonathon's expression was so blank, so unchanging she thought he might have suffered a stroke.

"I—" he began. Then he looked down at Peyton, his frown deepening. "Well—" He looked back at her and cocked his head to the side. "It turns out Jeanell was right. On-site childcare was a good idea. I'm sure she'll be just fine there."

Dread settled in Wendy's belly. As well as something else. Sorrow. Nostalgia maybe. She didn't want to leave FMJ. Even though she was just an assistant here, she'd never felt more at home anywhere else. Professionally or personally. Working at FMJ had given her purpose and direction. Something her family had never understood.

"I'm not going to bring Peyton to work," she began.

And then decided there was no point in pussyfooting around this. "I'm not coming to work anymore. I came in today to resign."

Two

"Don't be ridiculous," Jonathon barked, too shocked to temper the edge of his words. "Nobody quits a job because they have a baby, much less because they inherited one."

Wendy rolled her eyes in exasperation. "That's not—" she started, but he held up a hand to cut her off.

"I know how stupid that sounded." This was why he needed Wendy. Why she was irreplaceable. Most of the time, he was too outspoken. Too blunt. Too brash. He had a long history of pissing off people who were easily offended. But not Wendy. Somehow, she managed to see past his mistakes and overlook his blunders.

The thought of trying to function without her here as his buffer made him panic. He wasn't about to lose her over a baby.

"FMJ has one of the highest-rated on-site child-care facilities in the area. There's no reason why you can't continue to work here."

"I can't work here because I have to move back to Texas." As she spoke, she crossed to the supply closet in the corner. She moved a few things around inside and pulled out an empty cardboard box.

"Why on earth would you want to move to Texas?"

She shot him another one of those looks. "You know I'm from Texas, right?"

"Which is why I don't know why you'd want to move back there. I've never once heard you say anything nice about living there."

She bobbed her head as if in concession of the point. Then she shrugged. Rounding to the far side of the desk, she sank into the chair and opened her drawer. "It's complicated."

"I think I can keep up."

"There's a chance members of my family won't want me to raise Peyton. Unless I can convince them I'm the best mother for her, there'll be a custody battle."

"So? You don't think you can win the battle from here?"

"I don't think I can afford to fight it." Sifting through things in the drawer, she answered without looking up. She pulled out a handful of personal belongings and dropped them into the open box.

He watched her for a moment, barely comprehending her words and not understanding her actions at all. "What are you doing?"

She paused, glancing up. "Packing," she said as if stating the obvious. Then she looked back into the drawer and riffled through a few more things. "Ford called yesterday to offer his condolences. When I explained, he said not to worry about giving two-weeks' notice. That if I needed to just pack up and go, I should."

Forget twenty-two years of friendship. He was going to kill Ford.

The baby squirmed. Wendy jostled her knee to calm the little girl, all the while still digging in the drawer. "I swear I had another tube of lip gloss in here."

"Lip gloss?" She'd just pulled the rug out from under him. If he'd had two weeks, maybe he could talk some sense into her. But no. His idiot of a partner had ripped that away too. And she was worried about lip gloss?

She must have heard the outrage in his voice, because her head snapped up. "It was my favorite color and they don't even make it anymore. And—" She slammed the drawer shut and yanked open another. "Oh, forget it."

"You can't quit."

She stood up, abandoning her task. "You think I want this? You think I want to move? Back to Texas? You think I want to leave a job I love? So that I can move home? I don't! But it's my only option."

"How will being unemployed in Texas solve anything?" he demanded.

"I…" Peyton squirmed again in her arms and let out a howl of protest. Wendy sighed, sank back into the chair and set it rocking with a pump of her leg. "I may not have mentioned it before, but my family has money."

She hadn't mentioned it. She'd never needed to.

People who grew up with money had an air about them. It wasn't snobbery. Not precisely. It was more a sense of confidence that came from always having the best of everything. It was the kind of thing you only noticed if you'd never had money and had spent your life trying to replicate that air of entitlement.

Besides, there was an innate elegance to Wendy that was in direct contrast to her elfin appearance and plucky verve. Yet somehow she pulled it off.

"From money?" he said dryly. "I never would have guessed."

Wendy seemed too distracted to notice his sarcasm. "My grandfather set up a trust for me. For all the grandkids, actually. I never claimed mine. The requirements seemed too ridiculous."

"And the requirements are?"

"I have to work for the family company and live within fifteen miles of my parents." She narrowed her eyes as if glaring at some unseen relative. Peyton let out another shriek of frustration and Wendy snapped back to the present. "So if I move home now—"

"You can claim the trust," he summed up. "You'd have enough money to hire a lawyer if it does come down to a custody battle."

"I'm hoping it won't come to that. My grandmother still controls the purse strings. The rest of the family will follow her wishes. Once she sees what a great mother I'm going to be, she'll back off and just let me raise Peyton." Wendy's jaw jutted forward in determination. "But if it does come to a custody battle, I want to be sure I have enough money to put up a good fight."

"I don't get it. You're doing all this for a cousin you barely knew? Someone you hadn't seen in years?"

Wendy's eyes misted over and for a second he thought that—dear God—she might actually start crying. She squeezed the baby close to her chest and planted a kiss on top of her head. Then she pinned him with a steady gaze brimming with resolution. "If something happened to Ford and Kitty, and they wanted you to take Ilsa, wouldn't you do whatever it took to honor their wishes?"

All he could do in response was shove his hands deep into his pockets and swallow a curse. Damn it, she was right.

He stared at the adorable tot on Wendy's lap, summing up his competition. He wasn't about to lose the best assistant he'd ever had. He didn't care how cute and helpless that baby was.

Peyton undoubtedly needed Wendy. But he needed her too.

Fighting the feeling of complete and utter doom—which, frankly, was a fight she'd been losing ever since the nanny had first handed her Peyton—

Wendy glanced from the baby, to the open desk drawer and then to Jonathon.

She had so much to do, her mind couldn't focus on a single task. Or maybe it was lack of sleep. Or maybe just an attack of nerves brought on by the way Jonathon kept pacing from one side of the room to the other, pausing occasionally to glower in her direction.

When she'd first started work at FMJ, Jonathon had made her distinctly nervous. There was something about his combination of magnetic good looks, keen intelligence and ruthless ambition that made her overly aware of every molecule of her body. And every molecule of his body for that matter. She'd spent the first six months on edge, jumping every time he came in the room, nearly trembling under his gaze. It wasn't nerves precisely. More a kind of tingling anticipation. As if she were a gazelle who wanted to be eaten by the lion.

She'd forced herself to get over it.

And she'd thought she'd been successful. Only now that feeling was back. Either she could chalk it up to exhaustion and emotional vulnerability. Or she could be completely honest with herself. It *wasn't* nerves. It was sexual awareness. And now that she was about to walk out of his life forever, she wished she'd acted on it when she'd had the chance.

Forcing her mind away from that thought, she stared at the open desk drawer. The lip gloss was gone forever, just like any opportunity she might have had to explore a different kind of relationship with Jonathon. The best she could hope for now was to gather her few remaining possessions and make a run for it.

She had a Voldemort for President coffee mug in the bottom drawer, her Bose iPod dock, a tub of Just Fruit strawberries and in the very back, a bag of Ghirardelli chocolate caramels. Precious few possessions to be walking away with after five years, and the cardboard box dwarfed them. On the bright side, at least she'd only have to make one trip out to the car.

Balancing Peyton on her hip, she wedged the box under her arm only to find Jonathon blocking her route to the door.

"You can't go."

"Right. The car seat. I can't believe I forgot that." She turned back around, only to notice the diaper bag as well.

She blew out a breath. Okay. More than one trip after all.

"No," Jonathon said. "I'm not letting you quit."

Turning back around, she stared at him. "Not letting me? How can you not let me? If I quit, I quit."

"You're the best assistant I've ever had. I'm not going to lose you over something this…" He seemed to be searching for the least offensive word. "Frivolous."

She raised an eyebrow. "She's a child, not a frivolity. It's not like I'm running off to join the circus."

There was something unsettling about the quiet, assessing way he studied her. Then he said, "If keeping this baby is really so important to you, we'll hire a lawyer. We'll find the best lawyer in the country. We'll take care of it."

She felt her throat tighten, but refused to let the tears out of the floodgate. Oh, how tempting it was to accept his help. But the poor man had no idea what he was getting into.

"You should know, my family is extremely wealthy. If they fight this, they'll put considerable financial and political weight behind it."

"So?"

She blew out a long breath. The moment of reckoning. She always dreaded this. "Leland is my mother's maiden name. I legally took her name when I left college."

Jonathon didn't look impatient, the way some people did when she explained. That was one of the things she liked best about Jonathon. He reached conclusions quickly, but never judgments.

"My father's name—" Then she corrected herself. "My *real* last name is Morgan."

Most people, it took a couple of minutes for them to put together the name Morgan with wealth and political connections. She figured as smart as he was, it would take Jonathon about twenty seconds. It took him three.

"As far as I know, none of the banking Morgans live in Texas. That means you must be one of the Texas oil Morgans."

He didn't phrase it as a question. His tone had gone flat, his gaze distant.

"I am." She bit her lip, not bothering to hide her cringe. "I should have told you."

"No. Why would you have?" His expression was so blank, so unsurprised, so completely disinterested, that it was obvious, at least to her, that he cared deeply that she'd kept her true identity to herself. His calm, direct gaze met hers. "Then Senator Henry Morgan is…"

"My uncle." In the interest of full disclosure, she

nodded to the baby gurgling happily on her hip. "Peyton's grandfather."

"Okay then." He stood with his hands propped on his hips, the jacket of his suit pushed back behind his hands. He often stood in that way and it always made her heart kick up a beat. The posture somehow emphasized the breadth of his shoulders and the narrowness of his waist all at the same time.

Despite his obvious disappointment, he immediately went into problem-solving mode. He stared at her blankly, then left the room abruptly. A moment later he returned with a copy of the *Wall Street Journal.* He flipped the paper open, folded it in half and held it out to her. "So, Elizabeth Morgan is your cousin. The baby's mother."

It was an article about her death. The first Wendy had seen. She didn't need to read it to know what it would say. It would be carefully crafted. Devoid of scandal. Bitsy may have been an embarrassment but Uncle Hank would have called in favors to make sure the article met with his approval. That was the way her uncle did business, whether he was running the country or running his family.

Jonathon frowned as he scanned the article. His eyes crinkled at the edges as his face settled into what she thought of as his problem-solving expression. But if he could figure a way out of this one, then he was smarter than even she thought he was.

"It says here she is survived by a brother and sister-in-law. Why don't they take the baby?"

"Exactly," she said grimly. "Why not? It's what every conservative in the country will be thinking. Those conservative voters made up a huge portion of Uncle Hank's constituents." And they weren't the only ones who had that question. It was no secret that their grandmother, Mema, didn't approve of modern families. In her mind, a family comprised a mother and a father. And possibly a dog. Mema would want Hank Jr. to take Peyton. And what Mema wanted was generally what the family did.

She may have been in her late eighties, but she was a wily old dame. More importantly, she still controlled the money.

"It's so frustrating," she admitted. "This wouldn't even be an issue if I had a husband I could trot out to appease my grandmother and Uncle Hank's constituents."

"You really think that's all you need?"

"For my family to see me as the perfect mother?" She gave a fake, trilling laugh. "Oh, yes, a husband is the must-have accessory of the season. The richer, the better. Optional add-ons are the enormous gas-guzzling SUV, the Junior League membership and the golden Lab."

"And it's really that simple?"

"Oh, sure. *That* simple. I'll just head over to the laboratory and whip up a successful husband out of spare computer parts. You run out to the morgue and steal a dead body I can reanimate and we'll be good."

His lips quirked in a smile, his eyes crinkling at the corners, just a hint of cockiness. The expression gave her pause, because he wasn't laughing at her joke. No, she knew this look too. It was his I've-solved-the-problem look. "I think we can do a little better than that."

"Excuse me?"

"You said it yourself. All you need is a rich, successful husband."

For a moment she just stared blankly at him, unable to follow the abrupt twist the conversation had taken. "Right. A rich, successful husband. Which I don't have."

"But you could." He smiled fully now. Full smiles were rare for him. Usually they made her feel a little breathless. This one just made her nervous. "All you have to do is marry me. I'll even buy you a dog."

Three

Having never before asked a woman to marry him, Jonathon wasn't quite sure what reaction he expected, but it wasn't Wendy's blank-faced confusion. Or maybe that was a perfectly normal reaction under the circumstances. After all, it wasn't every day a man proposed to his assistant for such transparently selfish reasons.

For a long moment, she merely stared at him, her blue-violet eyes wide, her perfect bow mouth gaping open in surprise.

She wasn't just surprised. She was disconcerted. His proposal had shocked her. Maybe even offended her. On some deeply intimate level, the thought of marriage to him horrified her.

Not that he could really blame her. Despite his wealth, he was no prize.

She was going to say no, and he couldn't let her do it.

He needed her. Quite desperately, if the past seven days had been any indication.

"I'm not proposing a romantic relationship," he reassured her, hoping to make his proposal seem as benign as possible.

"Obviously," she muttered. Still holding the baby in her arms, she sank to the edge of the desk. She dipped her head, nuzzling the tuft of dark hair on Peyton's head.

"This would be strictly a business arrangement." He argued more vehemently as he felt her slipping away. "We'll stay married as long as it takes to convince your family that we're suitable parents. We won't even have to live together. I'll grant you an annulment as soon as we've convinced them."

"No," she said softly.

He felt a pang in his chest at her response. Then he saw it. Her letter of resignation. Signed, dated and ready to be handed over. As official as an order for his execution.

This past week had been a premonition of his future without her. He could envision an endless parade of incompetent temps. Countless hours of interviewing assistants, all of whom would fail to live up to the precedent set by Wendy. This government contract would slip through his fingers, just as the Olson deal had. FMJ had lost millions on that one. Which was nothing compared to what they'd miss if they didn't secure this contract. He could feel the stepping-stone slipping out from under him, the future he'd planned out for the company dissolving before his very eyes.

Panic mounting, he kept talking. "If you're worried about sex, don't be. I certainly wouldn't expect to sleep with you."

Her gaze darted to his as she bolted to her feet. "No." Then she squeezed her eyes closed for an instant. "What I meant was..." She drew in a deep breath. "...a fast annulment wouldn't work."

Just as quickly, her eyes shifted away from his. In that moment, a powerful, unspoken message passed between them.

Not once in all the years they'd worked together had they talked about sex. They had shared countless other intimacies. Eaten meals late at night. Sat beside each other on long plane flights. He'd had her fall asleep with her head on his shoulder somewhere over the Atlantic Ocean. They had slept in hotel rooms with walls so thin he'd heard the sound of her rolling over in her bed. And yet despite all that, neither of them had ever broached the subject of sex.

But now that the word had been said aloud, it was there between them. The image of her, sprawled naked on a bed before him, was permanently lodged in his brain.

He found himself oddly pleased by the faint blush that crept into her cheeks as she couldn't quite meet his gaze.

"If we're going to do this—" she shot him a look from under her lashes as if she were trying to assess his commitment "—then we have to go all in."

He raised his eyebrows, speculatively. She wasn't saying no. She was making a counteroffer. He felt a grin split his face. Just when he thought he knew her, she always managed to surprise him.

"We can't get an annulment in three or even six months," she said. "My family will see right through that. In a year, maybe two, we'll have to get divorced. Simply pretend the marriage didn't work out."

"I see."

She shook her head. "I don't think you do. I'm

committed to fighting for Peyton. I'll do whatever I have to. But I can't ask you to do the same."

"You're not asking," he pointed out. "I'm offering. And just so we're clear, I'm not doing this out of the goodness of my heart." The last thing he needed right now was her developing some starry-eyed notion about his motives. "I'm doing this to keep you working for FMJ. You're the best damn assistant I've ever had."

She threw up her hand to interrupt him. "This is ridiculous. Just hire another assistant. I'll even help you find one. There are plenty of other competent people in the city."

"But none of them are you. I need you," he argued. "None of them know the company the way you do. None of them would care about what FMJ does the way you do."

She seemed to be considering for a moment, then admitted, "Well, that's true."

"Besides. I don't have the time or energy to train someone new. My motives are very selfish."

"Trust me, I wasn't about to swoon from the romanticism of the moment." Her lips twisted in a wry smile. "I just want to make sure you know what you're getting into. If my family suspects what we're up to—"

"Then we'll convince them that our marriage has nothing to do with Peyton."

Her eyebrows shot up. "Convince them we're in love?"

"Exactly."

Wendy gave a snort of laughter. Baby Peyton squirmed in response. She turned her head and gave Jonathon a look of annoyance. If a baby could be annoyed. Obviously she wasn't going back to sleep. Pressing her tiny palms to Wendy's chest, she pushed away as if she wanted to be set free.

Wendy crossed to a diaper bag sitting on her desk. He hadn't even noticed it before, but when Wendy tried to unzip it with one hand, he moved to help her. He brushed her fingers aside and unzipped the bag. "What do you need?"

"The blanket. That pink one there. Spread it out on the floor."

Once the blanket was out, she situated the baby on her belly in the center of it.

The sight of a baby in the middle of FMJ's executive offices was so incongruous he could barely remember what they'd been talking about. Oh, right. She'd been snorting with laughter over the idea of them being in love. Nice to know he'd amused her.

"So you don't think we can convince your family we're romantically involved?"

Wendy was back at the diaper bag now, pulling out an array of brightly colored toys. "No offense, Jonathon, but in the five years I've been here, I don't think I've ever seen you romantically involved."

"That's ridiculous. I—"

She held up her hands to ward off his protests. "With anyone. Oh, I know you've dated *plenty* of women." She stressed "plenty" as if it was an insult. "But romance is not your strong suit."

Dropping to her knees, she strategically placed the toys in an arc in front of the baby. By now, Peyton had wedged herself up on her elbows.

"You think I can't be romantic?" he asked.

"I think you approach your love life with all the warmth and spontaneity of a long-term strategic planning committee."

"You're saying...what? That I'm a cold fish?" His voice came out tight and strained.

There was something very matter-of-fact about her tone. As if she were stating the obvious. As if it hadn't even occurred to her that this might insult him.

"Not really." She tilted her head to the side, her attention focused on Peyton. She nudged a stuffed elephant closer to the baby. He didn't know if the topic made her uncomfortable or if infant toys were really just that fascinating. "More that you keep your emotions tightly under control." Apparently satisfied with the arrangement of toys, she stood, dusting her hands off. "You're a dispassionate man. There's nothing wrong with—"

Okay, he'd had enough. He strode toward her, pulled her into his arms and kissed her.

He didn't know what pushed him over the edge. Whether it was her unending lecture about how dispassionate he was. Or the fact that ever since he'd said the word "sex" aloud a few minutes ago he hadn't been able to get it out of his head. Or maybe it was that tempting bit of shoulder her shirt kept exposing. Or hell, maybe it was even the hot-pink strap.

Whatever it was, his restraint snapped and he had to kiss her. And then, he couldn't stop.

Wendy had not seen it coming. One minute, she was trying to calm Peyton down, keep her distracted enough so she could keep talking to Jonathon. Because frankly, Wendy was having enough trouble concentrating on the logistics of the conversation without Peyton breaking out into all-out fussiness.

And then, a second later, her body was pressed against Jonathon's and his mouth was moving over hers in a kiss heaven made to knock her socks off.

One hand cradled her jaw, his fingertips rough against the sensitive skin of her cheek. The other was wrapped firmly around her waist, his hand strong against her back, pressing her so close to him she could feel the buttons of his shirt through the thin cotton of her T-shirt.

His kiss was completely unexpected. When he had crossed the room to her, the lines of his face taut, his expression so full of intent, it had never occurred to her that he was going kiss her.

Sure, in the past, she'd imagined what it might be like to kiss him. After all, they'd worked side by side for years. Just because she had a modicum of restraint didn't mean she was dead. Despite the pure perfection of his exterior, she'd always imagined that in the bedroom Jonathon was very much how he was in the boardroom. Analytical. Logical. In control. Dispassionate.

Holy guacamole, had she been wrong.

His lips didn't just kiss hers. They devoured her.

She felt his tongue in her mouth, stroking hers, coaxing a response, all but demanding she participate, until she found herself rising up onto her toes and wrapping her arms around his neck, brushing her palm against the bristle of soft hair on the back of his head.

The kiss was hot and endless. He tasted faintly of coffee and fresh minty toothpaste and deeply buried longing. He stirred feelings within her that she'd never even imagined. And she could just not get close enough to him.

He backed her up a step. And then another. She felt the edge of her desk bump against the back of her legs. And still he pressed into her, bending her so her back arched.

An image flashed through her mind of him sweeping the desk clear, pressing her down onto her desk and taking her right there. The idea came to her so completely, it was as though it had been right there in the back of her mind for years. Just waiting for his kiss to pull it out of her.

There was no one else in the building. Why shouldn't they give in to this thing between them? She couldn't think of a single reason not to.

She still hadn't thought of one a moment later when he pulled his mouth from hers and stepped away. He cleared his throat, then tugged down the hem of his jacket to straighten it.

He left her aching for him. Missing the warmth

of his body, even though he was only a foot away. Wishing she had some idea of why he'd kissed her. Why he'd stopped…

Peyton.

Oh, crap. Peyton!

Wendy looked past Jonathon to where Peyton still lay on her belly on the floor.

Holy guacamole, indeed! She'd been a mother for less than four days and she'd already abandoned her daughter on the floor to make out with her boss. Maybe her family was right. Maybe she really was unfit to be Peyton's mother.

Her gaze sought Jonathon. He'd crossed to the other side of the room so that Peyton lay between them like a landmine.

He ran a hand across his jaw, then shoved his hand deep in his pocket. She'd never seen him look quite so disconcerted. Though he still looked less shaken than she felt.

"Well," he began, then swallowed visibly. "I think we can both agree that if I need to I can convince your family that I am more than your boss."

"Yeah. I think so." Then she paused for a beat while his words sank in. "*That's* what this was about?" For a second, confusion swirled through her, muddling her thoughts even further. "You kissed me merely to make a point?"

"I—" He shrugged, apparently at a loss for words.

Indignation pushed past her embarrassment. "I was seconds away from dropping my panties to the floor and you were making a point?"

For an instant, his gaze fell to her feet as if imagining her panties lying there. He swallowed again as he dragged his gaze back to hers, then ran a hand down his face.

Well, at least she wasn't the only one whose world had been rocked.

"It seemed a prudent move," he said stiffly.

She nearly snorted her derision. Prudent? The kiss that had curled her toes all the way up to her kneecaps had seemed *prudent* to him?

"Oh, that is wrong in so many ways, I don't even know where to start."

He tried to interrupt her. "Actually—"

But she cut him off with a wag of her finger. "No, wait a second. I *do* know where to start. If you think offering to marry me for Peyton's sake gives you an all-access pass to this—" she waved her hand in front of her body "—then you have another think coming." He looked as if he might say something in protest, but she didn't give him a chance. "And secondly, you have no business kissing me merely to make a point."

And then—because she realized that was practically an invitation to kiss her for other reasons—she added, "In fact you have no business kissing me at all. If we're going to do this pretend-marriage thing, we need to set some boundaries. And thirdly…well, I have no idea what thirdly is yet, but I'm sure it will come to me eventually."

For a long moment, Jonathon merely stared at her, one eyebrow slightly arched, his lips curved to just hint at his amusement. "Are you done?"

She clamped her lips together, painfully aware of how cool and collected he seemed when she'd just been rambling like an idiot. A surefire sign that her emotional state was neither cool nor calm.

Maybe she was wrong about the kiss affecting him as much as it did her. And wouldn't that just suck. Didn't she have enough on her plate just now? This was so not the time for her to be nursing a crush on her boss. Or her husband.

When had her life gotten so complicated?

On the floor between them, Peyton wedged her tiny hands under her to push up onto her forearms. She let out an excited squeal of pride.

Right. This was when her life had gotten complicated. Approximately five days ago in her grandfather's study when the lawyer dropped Bitsy's will on her like a bomb.

Wendy let loose a sigh of frustration. "I'm sorry," she said. "None of this is your fault. I shouldn't take it out on you. I just—"

"I agree we need boundaries," he said abruptly, cutting her off before she could bumble further into the apology. His tone was stiff, as if he was searching for the most diplomatic way to broach the subject. "Keeping sex out of this is a good idea. However, kissing you now seemed prudent because we will have to kiss again at some point."

"We will?" she asked weakly, her gaze dropping to his mouth.

"Naturally."

She felt a curious heat stirring deep inside at the idea. He was going to kiss her again. Soon? She hoped so. Even if it was a very bad idea, she hoped so.

"If we're going to convince people we're in love and getting married, people will expect certain displays of affection."

"Oh, I hadn't thought..." Obviously, there was a lot she hadn't considered about this idea. She didn't know whether or not to be thankful that Jonathon's brain worked so much faster than her own. Was it a good thing he was around to consider things she hadn't? Or was it merely annoying to always be one step behind?

"The people who know us best will be hardest to convince. Luckily Ford and Matt will both be out of town for another few weeks. We'll have to get used to the idea ourselves before see them."

"Ford and Matt? Surely we don't need to lie to them?" Jonathon had been best friends with Ford and Matt since they were kids.

He leveled a steady gaze at her. There was no hesitation. No doubt. "Yes, we do. If your family decides to fight us on this, it could mean a court battle. I can't ask either of them to lie for us."

"Oh." Feeling suddenly weak, she sank back to the edge of the desk.

Of course they couldn't ask Ford and Matt to lie for them. In the five years she'd worked with FMJ, she'd served as executive assistant for all three men equally.

They worked so closely together they'd decided long ago it was easier to share one assistant among the three of them. Undoubtedly that was why they'd gone through so many assistants before she'd come along. Managing the schedules and needs of three such disparate men was no easy task. In short, she was a miracle worker.

If the thought of lying to them was this difficult for her, then how must Jonathon feel about the matter?

She propelled herself away from the desk and crossed to stand in front of him. Gazing up into his mossy-green eyes, she studied him. "This is a crazy and ridiculous plan. Are you sure you want to do this?"

His lips curved into a slight smile. His eyes lit with a reckless gleam as they crinkled at the corners, giving her the distinct impression that he was enjoying this. "Yeah. I'm sure. If there's one thing I know, it's how to make the strategic risk pay off."

The resolve in his gaze was as clear as the doubt probably was in her own. Then she looked down at where Peyton lay on the floor. She scooped up the precious little girl and held her close. This moment felt profound. As though she and Jonathon were striking a bargain that was going to change all of their lives. It seemed only right that Peyton be a part of it as well.

"Okay," she said. "Let's do this."

Jonathon's face broke into a full grin. He gave a brisk nod then spun on his heel, moving toward his office as he started barking orders, back into full boss mode.

"First off, email Ford and Matt and schedule another teleconference for later in the day. Then call Judge Eckhart and see if he has time in his schedule to perform the ceremony next Friday. Clear my schedule and yours for the following two weeks."

Wendy was used to having Jonathon rattle off a to-do list like this. Even trying to juggle Peyton, she kept up pretty well. Until he got to the last item on the list.

"Wait a second. Clear our schedules? What are we going to be doing? And what about the government contract?"

"We'll work on that this week. And we'll have another couple of weeks after we get back. It'll be tight, but I have no doubt we'll get it done."

"Get back? Get back from where?"

He paused by his desk and looked up at her, that cocky smile still on his face. "From our honeymoon."

"Our honeymoon?" Surprise pitched her voice high.

"Don't get too excited. We're just going to Texas.

If we're going to win this battle with your family, we need to go on the offensive. That means taking the fight to them."

Four

When Jonathon called her into the conference room the next morning, she was surprised to see Randy Zwack there. Randy had gone to college with Jonathon, Matt and Ford before going on to law school. He'd occasionally done work for FMJ, before they'd hired an intellectual property legal department, but that had been long before her time. She was more confused than surprised when she walked into the conference room and saw him there—looking more harried than usual.

Jonathon stood at the far end of the room, back to the door, staring out at the view of Palo Alto sprawling below. Randy sat dead in the center of the table, stacks of paper spread out before him. The lawyer looked up when she entered. He half stood and offered her a strained smile.

"Oh, good. You're here," he said as if he'd been waiting for her. "We can get started."

"Hi, Randy." She looked past him to Jonathon. When he turned around, she raised her eyebrows in question. "What's up?"

He frowned and with unusual hesitancy said, "I asked Randy here to draw up a prenuptial agreement for us." He held out a hand to ward off some protest he imagined she might make. "Don't worry. I trust his discretion."

"I'm not worried." In fact, delighted was more like it. "Calm down. I think a prenup is a fantastic idea."

"You do?" Randy looked surprised.

"Why wouldn't I?" She sat down in the chair opposite Randy. "I assume Jonathon told you why he's helping me?"

Randy gave a little nod, still looking suspicious.

"This is a marriage custom-made for a prenup."

"In the interest of full disclosure…" Randy ran a hand over his hair, which today looked disheveled, though it was normally meticulously styled to hide his growing bald spot. "This is not my area of expertise. I told Jonathon he should hire a good family lawyer, but—" Randy winced.

"But Jonathon can be very pig-headed."

"I was going to say determined."

No wonder the poor guy looked so disconcerted. Jonathon had obviously browbeat him into drawing up the prenup. And doing it on a very tight schedule, since Jonathon had proposed less than twenty-four hours ago.

"Don't worry." Wendy reached across the table and patted Randy's hand. "I'm sure you did great. It's all pretty cut-and-dry."

Jonathon took a few steps closer to loom over them from the end of the table. He'd shoved his hands into his pockets in that way she found so distracting.

This was the man who was going to be her husband. In less than a week. Her stomach tightened at the thought.

"Okay, let's see this puppy. It's just your standard prenup, right?"

Reaching for the stack of papers in front of Randy, she clapped her hands in a way that was overly cheerful, as if this was a big fake check from Publishers Clearinghouse. But neither man noticed. Randy was too busy sending Jonathon a pointed glance and Jonathon was too busy glaring Randy into intimidated silence. She looked from one man to the other.

"This *is* a standard prenup? Right?"

Jonathon cleared his throat and loomed some more.

"You have nothing to worry about. Any assets you bring to the marriage or inherit while married revert to you upon the absolution of the union." Randy flushed bright as he spoke. Just in case she'd seen through his obfuscation.

Ignoring Jonathon, she looked pointedly at Randy, waiting for him to cave. "That's not what I asked, now, is it?"

He cleared his throat. "You…um…have nothing to worry about."

"Yes, you said that already. What about him?" She nodded in Jonathon's direction.

"The prenup was written to my specification," Jonathon said tightly. "I'm satisfied."

Which was not the same thing at all.

Randy blushed all the way to his receding hairline, but refused to look at her. Jonathon, on the other hand, met her gaze without even flinching, which actually made her more nervous.

"Give me a minute." Neither man budged. "Alone. With the prenup." Still no movement from the united front. "Either you give me time to read it or you—"

she pointed at Randy "—tell me what it is he doesn't want me to see."

Randy looked to Jonathon, who glowered at her for a second before granting a tight nod. Randy pulled her copy closer and flipped to a page midway through.

She scanned the paragraph, then read it aloud to give voice to her exasperation. "In the event of separation, annulment or divorce, the following premarital assets belonging to Jonathon Bagdon shall transfer to Gwendolyn Leland—the monetary value of twenty percent of all real property, tangible property, securities and cash owed by—"

She broke off in frustration, too stunned to continue. She glared at them both. "Whose idea was this ridiculous clause?"

Randy held up his hands. "Not mine." He sounded as offended as she was.

"But you *let* him include this? Are you insane?" She clenched and unclenched her fingers around the pen Randy had handed her as he gave a what-could-I-do shrug. She smiled tightly at him and said through clenched teeth, "Will you please give me a minute alone with my future husband?"

Randy skittered away like a death-row inmate given a pardon. She didn't blame him. Someone was going down. She wouldn't want to get caught in the crossfire either.

The second they were alone she asked, "Twenty percent? Twenty? Are you crazy?"

Jonathon at least had the good sense to try to sound placating. "Now, Wendy…"

"You know I'm not taking twenty percent!"

"After two years being married to me, you may think you've earned it."

She blew out a breath of exasperation. "I'm not taking. A penny. Of your money."

"Don't forget, California is a community property state. If you don't sign the prenup, you're entitled to half of anything I earn while we're together. For all you know that could be more than this twenty percent."

"What? Because you haven't been meeting your full potential before now?" He just scowled at her. "You know that has nothing to do with why I'm marrying you."

"I also know exactly how much money you make and that you'll have trouble supporting yourself and a child on that income."

"Lots of single-parent families get by on what I make," she pointed out.

"Maybe they do," he countered. "But you don't have to."

"So what? You're just going to give me all of that money? Did you somehow miss the conversation yesterday where I mentioned that I'm a Morgan? Trust me when I tell you, Jonathon, I will be fine."

His lips curved into the barest hint of a smile. "No. I didn't miss that, but I also know how damn stubborn you are. And I know that you're not going to ask your family for money. If you were the kind of person who would do that, you wouldn't be in this position to begin with."

Hmm. Good point. "But," she countered, "you thought you'd talk me into taking twenty percent of your assets?"

"No. I rather hoped you'd sign the prenup without noticing that part."

Well, that she could believe. He was just arrogant enough to think he could get away with a stunt like that.

"Even if I *had* signed the papers, I still wouldn't have taken the money. That's almost—" She struggled to do the math. Jonathon, no doubt, knew exactly how much that was, to the dime, at any given moment. "That's…tens of millions of dollars." Certainly more than the trust she'd never bothered to claim, which was a measly eight million. "I'm not taking that kind of money from you."

He shrugged dismissively. "It's a drop in the bucket."

"It's a fifth of the bucket. That's a lot of drops." She forced out a long. slow breath. Why was she angry? Why exactly?

She put voice to her thoughts as they came to her, not willing to give herself time to soften them. "Look, you've always been arrogant and controlling."

He raised his eyebrows. Probably in surprise that she'd say it aloud to him. He certainly couldn't be shocked by the idea.

"At work, it's fine," she continued. "You're my boss. But if we're going to get married, then the second we walk out that door each day—" she jabbed a finger toward the door "—you have to stop trying to control everything. Even if this isn't a real marriage."

"Wendy, I'm not—"

"But you are," she said, cutting him off. "Don't you get it? If I wanted to sit back and be taken care of for the rest of my life, I never would have left Texas. I *like* having to work for a living. I've been rich. I know that money alone won't make me happy.

And I also know that being with someone who's always trying to control me will make me miserable. So either you back off, or we walk away from this now."

He stared at her a long time, his gaze hard-edged and steely. She didn't back down. She couldn't. Her gut told her that if she lost her foothold now, she wouldn't recover. Besides, she was far too used to intimidating glares from her father or uncle to do that. Eventually, she even smiled. "See. Your Jedi mind tricks don't work on me."

His lips twitched at her comment and finally, he gave a terse, reluctant nod, as if agreeing to keep his own money was an affront to his personal honor.

"There's something else you should know."

"Okay, hit me."

"In the event of my death, you and Peyton get it all." She opened her mouth to protest, but he raised a hand to cut her off. "I'm not budging on that one."

"What about your family?" As familiar as she was with his schedule, she knew he didn't see them often, but they did exist. "Surely you want them to have your fortune."

His eyes were dark and shuttered. His face nearly expressionless. "There are certain charitable organizations that I've already provided for. If I die while we're married, I want you to have the rest."

She studied him for a moment. Since this was the most she'd ever heard him say about his family—precisely nothing—she had to assume he was serious. Boy, and she thought her relationship with her family was screwed up. "Okay," she said softly. "Then we'll just have to take very good care of you for the next two years. Make sure you take your vitamins." She smiled at her own joke, but he didn't return the smile. "Now that that's settled, I'll go tell Randy he can do his job and protect his client."

She'd almost made it out the door when Jonathon's words stopped her.

"I don't want you to fall in love with me."

Hand already on the doorknob, she turned to face him, eyebrows raised. "Excuse me?"

His expression was so strained as to be nearly comical. "If we're going to be together a year or maybe two, I don't want you imagining that you've fallen in love with me."

Fighting back a chuckle, she searched his face, but saw no signs that he was joking. In fact, he looked so serious, it made her heart catch in her chest. She had to force a teasing smile. "Why? Because you're so charming and charismatic that I won't be able to be constantly in your company without falling in love?" He didn't smile at her, so she asked, "Is this a separate issue from the money or are the millions of dollars supposed to ease my heartache if I did fall in love with you?"

His lips twitched again, but she wasn't sure if it was with suppressed humor or irritation. "Separate issue. But I'm serious."

She could certainly see that. It made her uneasy, but she couldn't say why. It wasn't arrogance—his fear that she might fall in love with him. No, despite his natural confidence, she didn't see that in his gaze now. Instead, she saw only concern. For her.

"Let me guess. You're not the type of man who believes in love." She could imagine that all too easily. Jonathon may feel physical passion—he'd proven that clearly enough when he'd kissed her yesterday—but love was something else entirely.

But to her surprise, he shook his head. "Oh, I believe in love. I know exactly how crippling it can be. That's why I don't want you to imagine you've fallen in love with me."

"Okay," she said, torn between wanting to reassure him, without telling him outright that she had absolutely no intention of risking her heart. Finally, she made the only counteroffer she could think of. "Then don't fall in love with me either."

He studied her for a moment, slowly smiling.

Her chin bumped up a notch. "What? You think you're above falling in love with me? I'll have you know I'm very loveable." Arching an eyebrow, she said, "I'm cute. And plucky. Greater men than you have fallen in love with me."

"I'm sure they have."

"You think I'm joking?" she demanded, all fake belligerence.

"Not for a minute," Jonathon conceded. And the really pathetic things was, he was being honest. In this moment, watching her trying to cajole him into laughing, it was all too easy to imagine falling in love with her. Smart, funny, never taking herself too seriously. Wendy was the whole package. Men who wanted things like a wife and family were probably waiting in line for a woman like her. Too bad he wasn't one of them.

"Just don't forget why I'm doing this. This isn't a favor to you. This isn't because I'm a nice guy. Don't romanticize me. Don't forget, not even for a minute, why I'm here. Why I'm doing this."

She looked up at him, her eyes wide, her expression suddenly serious but a little bemused, as if she had no idea where he was going with this. "Remind me then. Why are you doing this?"

He was struck—not for the first time—that she wasn't merely cute, but truly beautiful. With her swoopy little button nose and her pixie dimples, her face had more than its share of cuteness. But she was also lovely, with her dark—almost violet—blue eyes and her luminous skin. Her beauty had an ephemeral quality to it. Like a woman in a Maxfield Parrish painting.

He was so struck by her beauty that for a second, he forgot her question. Forgot that he was trying to direct this conversation. To remind her that he wasn't some hero.

"I'm doing this for the same reason I've done everything else since I was eleven. I'm doing this because it serves my own goals. It serves FMJ."

She gave him an odd look, as something almost like pity flickered across her expression. "If you didn't want me to romanticize you, then maybe you shouldn't have tried to give me a big nasty chunk of your fortune. So I'm going to reserve the right to think you're not the heartless bastard you pretend to be."

"You have to believe me when I tell you that everything I've done for you was for my own benefit.

Keeping you in California was the best thing for FMJ. Marrying you is the best thing for FMJ. That's the only reason I'm doing it."

Finally she nodded. "Okay. If you want to keep insisting you're so coldhearted, then I'll try to remind myself as often as possible. We'll start with the prenup, okay? We'll ask Randy to rewrite it so I have to pay you twenty percent of my money. How does that sound?" She smiled as she asked, but it looked strained.

"Wendy—" he started.

"At the very least, we'll put Randy out of his misery. We'll go with the bare-bones prenup. Everyone walks away with what they had when they came into the marriage."

He sighed. It wasn't what he wanted. Not by a long shot. But he was starting to realize that when it came to Wendy, he wasn't ever going to get what he wanted.

She paused at the door and looked over her shoulder, her forehead furrowed in thought. "The thing is, Jonathon, if you really were a heartless bastard, you wouldn't have warned me off."

Five

The next few days passed in a blur of planning and activity. Wendy often felt as if her life was moving at double time while she was stuck at half speed. She'd felt like that ever since she'd gotten that fateful call about Bitsy, less than two weeks before. Her shock and grief were finally beginning to recede into the background. Though she no longer faced the daunting challenge of moving back to Texas, agreeing to marry Jonathon had created even more turmoil in her life.

True to his word, Jonathon managed to cram in considerable work on the proposal for the government contract, delegating things he normally would have handled himself. Ford and Kitty flew home immediately with their daughter, Ilsa. Matt and Claire arrived a few days later, having cut short their honeymoon, something Wendy still felt bad about. Claire insisted that seventeen days in a tropical paradise was enough for anyone and that she wouldn't miss the wedding for anything. Her reassurances didn't make Wendy feel any less guilty.

The Sunday before the wedding, she was still half-asleep watching a rerun of *Dharma & Greg* wishing Peyton seemed half as drowsy. Jonathon had eventually convinced her that she should move into his house. Since they were planning on being married for a year or more, he pointed out that people were unlikely to believe they were truly in love if they weren't living together. The night before she'd pulled out her trusty suitcase and hoped to pack the bare essentials once Peyton fell asleep. If she could stay awake herself. She'd leave her other belongings for some later date.

She hadn't slept well since…well, since taking Peyton, and her exhaustion was creeping up on her. Frankly, it had been all she could do to drag herself out of bed this morning. The middle-of-the-night feedings were just not her thing. She was sitting on the sofa, blearily rocking back and forth, wondering if she could get Babies "R" Us to deliver a rocking chair by the end of the day, when the doorbell rang.

It was a bad sign that it took her so long to identify the noise.

She set the bottle down on the side table, stumbled to her feet and pried the door open, praying that no one on the other side would expect coherent conversation.

She frowned at the sight of Kitty and Claire. She'd only known Claire for seven months, but the concern lining the other woman's face was obvious in the crinkle between her brows. As if to distract from her frown, she thrust forward a pink bakery box with the Cutie Pies logo stamped on the top.

"We brought food!" Claire announced, her tone overly chipper. "We just flew in from Palo Verde this morning. I made this batch just before I left."

Claire owned a diner in the small town of Palo Verde, a couple of hours away. Jonathon, Ford and Matt had grown up in Palo Verde. If Claire had baked whatever was in the box, she couldn't wait to dive in. And if fate was kind at all, the box would be filled with the spicy, dark chocolate doughnuts that the diner was known for.

Kitty gave Wendy a once-over, then announced, "Since you're obviously too tired to invite us in, why not just step aside." She held out her hands. "Here, hand me the baby. You take the doughnuts. Please, eat some before I fight you for them."

Mutely, Wendy handed the fussy Peyton over to Kitty.

Kitty Langley was the kind of woman who looked as if she didn't have a maternal bone in her body. The jewelry-store-heiress-turned-jewelry-designer had lived in New York until falling in love with and marrying Ford the previous year. How that woman could look glamorous while cradling a baby in her arms, Wendy didn't know. But she did envy the skill, since she was pretty sure she herself looked as if she was recovering from the flu.

Wendy happily traded baby for doughnuts.

Though her arms ached from the hours of holding Peyton, the bone-deep weariness melted a bit as she sank her teeth into the dense buttermilk doughnut.

"I'm not sure why you came," she muttered past a mouthful of heaven. "But, frankly, I no longer care. You can hold me at gunpoint. Rob me. Even take the baby. Just leave the doughnuts and I'll be happy."

Kitty stifled a smile as she pressed her bright red lips to the crown of Peyton's head. "You're in that too-exhausted-to-be-tired stage, aren't you?"

After a few minutes of being held by Kitty, Peyton

stopped fussing long enough to put her head down on Kitty's shoulder. And then there was silence. Peyton's eyes drifted closed and she exhaled a slow, shaky breath. Then her back settled into the gentle rhythm of sleep.

Tension seeped out of every pore in Wendy's body.

"Oh, thank goodness," she muttered.

Claire smiled wryly. "Did you get any sleep at all last night?"

"A couple of hours here and there," she admitted. "This caring for a baby gig is way harder than I expected."

"Oh, honey, you said a mouthful there." Kitty gave a low whistle, no doubt remembering her own new-to-mothering days. Walking with an exaggerated sway, Kitty crossed to the bassinet, so she could lay the baby down. "And at least I had seven months to get used to the idea."

The room fell silent as Kitty eased the sleeping Peyton down. Claire trotted off to the kitchen and returned a few minutes later with a steaming cup of coffee. "With cream and sugar," she said as she handed it over. "I assume all sane people take it that way."

Wendy took a grateful sip as Kitty asked, "Can we get you anything else? Something to eat maybe? I can't cook worth a damn, but Claire could McGyver a feast out of the barest cupboard."

Wendy didn't doubt it. "I think I'll save room for another doughnut."

"You sure?" Claire asked, in hushed tones so as not to wake the baby. "I could whip up an omelet. Or something else? I saw some nice Gouda in the fridge when I was foraging for cream." With a smile she added, "I could make you a grilled cheese sandwich so good you'll cry."

"No, thank you."

"You should try the grilled cheese," Kitty urged. "It's amazing."

"No, really. I'm okay." Wendy looked from Kitty to Claire, suddenly suspicious. "Why do I get the feeling I'm being plied with food for nefarious reasons?"

Kitty and Claire exchanged a look.

Wendy raised an eyebrow. "Come on, spill. What's up?"

Claire's cheeks reddened with what Wendy could only assume was guilt. Kitty played her cards closer to her chest. Her expression revealed nothing.

"Okay, obviously you have some bad news for me. Either that or you're going to try to get me to join a cult. Which is it?"

Claire bit down on her lip, her chin jutting out at a rebellious angle.

Kitty gave a little eye roll and sighed with obvious exasperation. “Fine,” Kitty said, managing to flounce a bit while sitting almost perfectly still. “We’re worried about Jonathon.”

Wendy gave a little grunt of surprise and sat back against the sofa. “Worried? About Jonathon?”

“Whatever is going on between you and Jonathon,” Claire began, “obviously has something to do with Peyton.”

Wendy opened her mouth to protest, but Kitty didn’t give her a chance.

“Jonathon wouldn’t talk about it, so I assume you won’t either. That’s fine. But we’re not idiots. Don’t forget, you told Ford why you were resigning just twenty-four hours before you and Jonathon announced you were getting married. If I had to guess, I’d say you’re pretending to be some happily married couple so your family will let you keep Peyton.”

Well, so much for hiding the truth from their friends.

“As convoluted and bizarre as that seems,” Kitty continued. “We’re not going to try to stop you.”

“We’ll even play along,” Claire added in. “Anything you need from us, you’ve got.”

"But when you're off playing house together, just be very careful."

For a long moment, Wendy had no idea what to say. She turned away from their careful scrutiny and walked over to the bassinet where Peyton lay sleeping.

She thought about the conversation she'd had with Jonathon before they'd signed the prenup. Apparently, he wasn't the only one who thought she was in danger of falling in love with him. And here she'd thought she'd hid her attraction to him so well over the years. Was she really so transparent?

Glancing back at Kitty and Claire, she forced a perky smile. "Look, I admit Jonathon is a great guy. I've always thought so. But I know his dating history probably better than either one of you. I know he doesn't open up easily. I'm not going to make the mistake of falling in love with him."

Claire and Kitty exchanged nervous glances, seeming to have an entire conversation with just their eyebrows.

"What?" Wendy demanded after a second, crossing back to the sofa to get a better view of their unspoken exchange.

Claire kept her mouth shut.

But it was Kitty who admitted, "Actually, it's him we're worried about."

Wendy sank back to the sofa. "You're worried about Jonathon? Falling in love with me?"

Claire nodded.

"Not me falling in love with him, but him. Falling in love. With me."

Kitty gave an elegant wave of her hand. "Obviously we don't want to see you left brokenhearted either. But you're a smart woman. Very practical. We just assumed you can look out for yourself."

"But you're worried that Jonathon, the brilliant, analytical CFO is going to get his feelings hurt?" Wendy fought back a giggle.

"Well," Claire hedged. "Yes."

Wendy looked from one woman to the other, her amusement fading. "You're serious?"

They nodded.

"I know that Jonathon seems…" Claire trailed off, searching for the right word.

"Detached," Kitty provided. "Ruthless."

Claire glared her into silence. "You're not helping."

"Like a heartless bastard," Wendy offered quietly.

"Yes!" Kitty agreed.

"But he really isn't," Claire said quickly. "Don't forget, I've known him longer than you have."

Which was technically true. Claire had grown up in the same small town as Matt, Ford and Jonathon. "But you're younger than he is. You didn't even go to school together."

"We overlapped some," Claire argued. "And I've seen him in love. Senior year, he was…" she trailed off, apparently struggling to convey the full force of his emotion. "He was just head over heels in love. Crazy in love with this girl. He would have done anything for her."

"Who was she?" Wendy found herself asking.

Claire hesitated. "Just a girl at school. Kristi hadn't grown up in Palo Verde. Her parents were divorced and she moved there to live with her dad her sophomore year."

"And they dated?"

"A little." Then Claire shrugged. "I think mostly he just chased her. She flirted a lot. He was completely determined to win her over. Any grand gesture you can imagine an eighteen-year-old guy making, he made it. Flowers, jewelry. The whole nine yards."

Flowers and jewelry? She knew he didn't have a lot of money growing up. He'd once told her he'd started saving money for college when he was twelve. She couldn't even imagine the man she knew taking money out of his precious college fund to buy gifts. For a girlfriend.

"Once," Claire said, leaning forward and warming up to the story, "she told him that her mother always bought her birthday cake from the same bakery. She'd grown up in San Francisco. So for her birthday, the guys made a road trip out to San Francisco to buy her a cake. On a school day. They got in so much trouble." Claire chuckled for a second. Then seemed to realize how much she'd revealed about herself. Her blush returned as she sank back against the sofa.

"You were a little bit of a stalker, weren't you?" Kitty asked, grinning.

"I had a crush on Matt. That's all." Then she smiled smugly. "Besides, he eventually came around."

"I'll say." Kitty bumped her shoulder against Claire's in easy camaraderie.

"So what happened?" Wendy asked, unwilling to leave the thread of Jonathon's story dangling. "Why did they break up?"

"That's the thing." Claire gave a little shrug. "I'm not sure they were ever really together. And not long after the birthday cake thing, she moved back in with her mother. Jonathon was…"

"Heartbroken," Kitty supplied.

"No." Claire frowned thoughtfully. "He was just never the same." She gave her head a little shake, as if she was returning to the present. "But I know it's still there, buried inside of him. The capacity to love like that."

Claire and Kitty exchanged another one of those pointed glances and Wendy felt a stab of envy. This girl he'd loved, Kristi… Wendy had never been loved like that. Kitty and Claire, that's what they had with their husbands. But no one had ever felt that way about Wendy.

She pushed herself to her feet. "I don't think you have to worry. He doesn't love me. I'm sure of it." She forced a bright smile. "You can go home and rest assured that I'm not going to crush his delicate heart beneath my boot heel."

"It's not just you we're worried about." Kitty stood also and looked across the room to the bassinet. "What about Peyton?"

"What about Peyton?"

"Have you ever seen Jonathon with Ilsa?" Kitty asked.

"I—" Then she broke off. Remembering that she had, once, seen him holding Ilsa. Right after she'd been born, Wendy had brought flowers by and Jonathon had been there, an expression of pure wonder on his face as he held the baby.

She nodded, rubbing at her temple, trying to dispel the tension headache that was spiking through her head. When had this all gotten so complicated?

"He's fantastic with kids," Kitty was saying. "He adores Ilsa. He's been bugging us to have another one in fact."

"And if you are getting married just to fool your family," Claire said. "And he falls in love with you or that darling little girl, how do you think he's going to feel when you end the marriage?"

"I—" What could she say to that? She'd never imagined Jonathon might fall in love with her. The idea was preposterous. But Peyton? Yeah. She could imagine that. And if they really were married for two years—it might take that long—then he'd have plenty of time for Peyton to wrap him around her tiny finger. She looked up at Kitty and Claire and found them watching her expectantly. "All I can say, is that when…*if* we get divorced, I wouldn't dream of keeping him away from Peyton. If he wants to see her, that is. From this moment on, I'll think of him as her father. Just as I think of myself as her mother."

Jonathon as a father. The idea was…so foreign.

So odd. Yet, she knew in her heart that Kitty and Claire were right to warn her. He was doing this amazing thing for her. She didn't want him to get hurt because of it and she would do everything in her power to make sure he didn't. She only wished she was half as confident in her ability to protect herself.

After a long moment, Kitty stood and gave a dramatic sigh.

"Very well, then. I suppose there's only one thing left to do."

"What's that?" Wendy asked, hesitantly.

Kitty's face broke into a smile. "Welcome you to the family."

Six

The wedding itself went off with all the precision of a well-planned military maneuver. And it was just about as romantic. A small ceremony performed in a drab municipal office in downtown Palo Alto, it was over so quickly that Jonathon felt sure Claire and Matt wished they had stayed in Curaçao instead of making the trip back.

After that first kiss in her office had gotten so out of control, he didn't even dare cement the ceremony with more than a quick peck. So much for convincing their friends that they were in love. But no one in the office that day seemed surprised, least of all Wendy.

That evening, they swung by Wendy's apartment

to pick up her suitcase and Peyton's few possessions before heading over to his house. They'd decided to keep her apartment for now. Her lease wasn't up for another few months, which would give her plenty of time to decide when she wanted to move into his house and what she wanted to keep in storage. When they arrived at his house, they discovered that Claire had made them dinner, and they found it waiting for them in the warming drawer of his kitchen.

He stood beside Wendy in the doorway to the kitchen, staring at the table with a fist clenching his heart. The table had been set with two of the elegant place settings his interior designer had bought seven years ago and which he'd never used. Long, thin tapers sat in the center of the table, a book of matches propped against the candle holder. In between the two chairs sat the new Svan high chair he'd had delivered. A bottle of unopened champagne sat chilling in a bucket opposite the high chair.

Wendy cleared her throat. "Um…" She hitched Peyton up on her hip. "I think I'll just…um…unpack a few of the bags first." Her gaze looked from the wine to him. "I'm not really hungry yet."

Before he could muster a response, she took the final suitcase from him and made a dash for the door. Probably a wise decision. Neither of them was ready yet for a intimate dinner. Let alone wine.

Three hours later, she still hadn't made it back down to eat. He'd sat at the table himself, eating in front of his laptop. Finally, he shut his laptop and went in search of Wendy. He found her upstairs in the room he'd set aside as a nursery.

He paused just outside the door. Leaning his shoulder against the doorjamb, for a long moment he simply watched her. The room had been painted pale pink. Butterflies fluttered across the walls and bunnies frolicked in the grass painted along the trim. A white crib sat in the corner under a mobile of more butterflies and flowers. Overall, the décor of the room was a little cloying in its sweetness, but the decorator had assured him that it was perfect for the new addition to his life. This evening, he barely noticed the butterflies, but rather focused his attention on the woman sitting in the rocking chair in the corner and the baby she held in her arms.

At some point, Wendy had changed out of the dress and into a pair of jeans and a white V-neck T-shirt. Peyton was asleep in her arms. Her eyes were closed, her head tilted back against the headrest of the rocking chair. Only the faint tensing of her calf as she occasionally nudged the chair into movement indicated that she wasn't asleep too.

He cleared his throat to let her know he was there.

Her head bobbed up. "Oh," she said, wiggling in the chair to reposition Peyton in her arms without waking her. "How long have you been there?"

"I just walked up."

She glanced down at the baby in her arms as Peyton stirred but didn't wake. "I suppose I should put her down," she whispered. "But I hate to do it. If she wakes up again…"

If the smudges of exhaustion under her eyes were any indication, Peyton wasn't the easiest of babies. No wonder given the upheaval in her young life.

"If she wakes back up," he found himself saying, "then I'll take over and you can get some sleep. You should go eat."

Wendy shook her head. "I can't ask you to do that. That's not why we got married."

There was almost a hint of accusation in her voice.

"Maybe not," he hedged. "But we are married now. And you obviously could use the sleep. At this point, I'm more rested than you are. A sleepless night won't hurt me, but a good night's sleep could do you a world of good."

"If she needs a bottle in the night—"

"Then I'll give it to her."

Wendy looked skeptical. "The bottles are downstairs. You just—"

"I saw you mixing the formula. I've got it."

"But—"

"Wendy, I'm one of five kids. I had a niece and two nephews before I graduated from high school. Peyton won't be the first baby I've ever fed."

"Oh." After a moment of hesitation, she stood and crossed to the crib.

As he'd told her, he knew his way around an infant. It was so obvious to him that she did not. There was a sort of fearful hesitancy to the way she moved. As if she were afraid of breaking Peyton.

She lowered the baby into the crib then stood there for a long moment, her hand resting on Peyton before she moved back a step. She cringed as she raised the side of the bed and the hardware clattered. But Peyton slept on and Wendy slowly backed away.

She paused as she closed the door to unclip the baby monitor from her hip and turn it on, as if Peyton might start crying any second and Wendy would miss it now that she was out of sight. He couldn't help chuckling when she raised the monitor to her ear to listen more closely.

She shot him an annoyed look. "What?"

"You know you're only one room away. You could probably hear her cry without the monitor." When she looked as if she might comment, he reached out and carefully extracted it from her fingers. "Not that you're going to need this tonight anyway."

"I really don't mind staying up with her."

"The discussion is over."

She opened her mouth to respond, then snapped it shut, her lips twisting into a smile. "I guess I know you well enough to recognize that I'm-the-boss-and-what-I-say-goes tone."

"I have a tone that says all that?"

She snorted her derision. "Yeah. And don't pretend you don't know it." She took a step in the direction of the room at the end of the hall—the guest room she'd claimed for her own—then she paused. "You didn't have to do this, you know."

"Wendy, let's not have another discussion about my motives."

She took another step toward him, closing the distance between them and lowering her voice. "No. I'm not talking about the wedding. I'm talking about all this." She nodded her head in the direction of Peyton's room. "I mean the nursery. The crib. The rocking chair. It's all—"

"It's nothing."

She quirked an eyebrow. "Like the twenty percent nothing? Unless you were up all night hand-painting butterflies and daisies last night, I'm guessing you hired an interior decorator to come in and do this. In less than a week. That's not nothing."

"Kitty mentioned that all you had was a bassinet."

She smiled a slow, teasing smile. "And you knew that wasn't enough. Being such an expert on babies and everything."

He was struck once again by the idea that this was their wedding night. That if there wasn't a baby asleep in the next room, he might now be slowly lifting that sweater up over her head. He might be unhooking that hot-pink bra of hers and stripping her naked.

But of course, if there wasn't a baby asleep in the next room, then there wouldn't have been a wedding to begin with. Let alone a wedding night.

Suddenly she reached up and cupped his jaw in her hand. Her gaze was soft, her touch gentle. "Thanks for taking such good care of us."

For a solid heartbeat—maybe longer—his brain seemed to completely stop working. He couldn't remember all the reasons why touching her was such a bad idea. All he knew was how much he wanted her. Not just in bed, but here. Like this. Looking up at him as if he was a decent guy who deserved a woman like her.

Before he could give in to the temptation to let her go on thinking that, he grabbed her hand in his and gently pulled it away from his face. Backing up a step, he said, "You should go to bed. Catch up on that sleep you've been missing."

He even used his I'm-the-boss tone.

"Right." She gave a chipper little salute. "Got it, boss."

Wendy had been so sure she wouldn't be able to sleep. She'd been positive she'd find herself waking at every sound coming from Peyton's room. She feared that she'd lie awake in bed thinking about the moment in the hall. But instead of the sleepless night she expected, she woke ten hours later to sun streaming in her bedroom window, feeling more rested than she had in weeks. Then she bolted upright in bed as panic clogged her heart. She'd slept through the night. Which meant she'd slept through Peyton waking and needing her God only knew how many times.

Wendy dashed down the hall and into Peyton's room, skidding to a halt beside the crib. It was empty. Her heart doubled its already accelerated rate. Where could—

"Morning."

She spun around to see Jonathon seated in the rocking chair, Peyton nestled on his lap as he fed her a bottle. Wendy pressed a hand to her chest, blowing out a whoosh of air, willing her heart rate to slow.

"You have her," she muttered. "She's fine."

Jonathon gave her a once-over, his gaze lingering on the tank top and boxers she always slept in. Finally his eyes returned to hers. "What did you think had happened to her?"

Wendy tugged at the hem of the thin white cotton, resisting the urge to glance down to verify just how thin the tank top was. She doubted knowing would bring her comfort. Instead she crossed her arms over her chest. "I don't know," she admitted. "It's the first morning in…what, almost three weeks now, that she hasn't been the one to wake me. For all I knew, she'd been abducted by aliens. I panicked."

His lips curved in an amused smile. "Obviously."

For a second she was entranced by the transformation of his face. He had a smooth, charming smile he used at work. She thought of it as his client-wooing smile. He also had a wolfish grin.

That was his I'm-about-to-devour-some-innocent-company expression.

Neither of those reached his eyes. Neither held any warmth.

But this slight, amused twist of his lips wrinkled the corners of his eyes, and it nearly took her breath away.

Before she could respond, or do something really stupid, like melt into a puddle at his feet, he continued. "Peyton and I have been up for hours now."

"I'm—"

"Don't apologize. I'd have woken you if she'd been any trouble."

Wendy's eyebrows shot up. When was Peyton not trouble? She fussed a lot. Wanted to be held constantly. Screamed anytime Wendy put her down. In general, made Wendy feel like a real winner as a parent.

"We got up a couple of hours ago," Jonathon was saying. He continued rocking as he spoke, looking down at Peyton the whole time. "She had her morning bottle. Then we made me some oatmeal. She sat on my lap while I read through some emails. She spit up a little on the office floor. Thank God for the plastic mat my chair sits on, right, Peyton?"

Oookay. Maybe that explained why his smile

looked so different than his normal grin. Obviously, it was Jonathon who'd been abducted by aliens and replaced by some sort of pod person. The man before her bore no resemblance to the cold and calculating businessman she'd dealt with for the past five years.

Unfortunately, this new guy was way more appealing, which was so annoying.

Jonathon looked up at her, his expression clouding with concern. "Anything wrong?"

"No, I… Why?"

"You looked a little, faint or something."

"No. I'm…great. Fantastic. But hungry. That's it. I must be hungry."

"Okay." The concern lining his brow had taken on a decidedly skeptical gleam. As though he suspected she might need to spend a little time in a padded room. "Why not get dressed and grab yourself some breakfast. Peyton and I will be fine here."

As if to signal her assent, Peyton blinked up at him with wide blue eyes, then gave the bottle a particularly vigorous suck before sighing and allowing her eyes to drift closed. She looked for all the world like a baby completely happy and at peace.

Emotion choked Wendy's throat, something that felt unpleasantly like envy. She'd worked her butt off for that baby over the past few weeks, turned her life upside down, prepared to battle her family to the end. And yet Peyton had never once looked up at her with dreamy contentment. Then again, Jonathon always had been quick to win over the ladies.

Wendy sighed. "I wish she was half as peaceful in my arms as she is with you."

"Why do you say that?"

Because if growing up a Morgan had taught her anything, it was that the best way to deal with negative emotions was to voice them aloud. Get them out into the open rather than letting them simmer. Still, admitting such a feeling was unpleasant, so she softened her words with a diffident shrug. "She seems to fight me constantly. Makes me wonder if—" Wendy blew out a breath. "I don't know, if she knows something I don't. If she knows I don't have what it takes to be a good mother."

When she looked back at Jonathon, his smile was still there, but the humor in his eyes had dimmed to understanding.

"The thing about dealing with babies—" he gently pulled the bottle nipple from Peyton's mouth, then maneuvered her so her belly rested against his shoulder "—it's about five percent instinct and ninety-five percent experience. Plus, they're very intuitive—

that's all they've got. So if you're nervous, she'll pick up on it and she'll be nervous too."

Jonathon gave Peyton's back several thumps. After about the tenth, she burped without even opening her eyes.

"How'd you do that? I can never get her to burp."

"Like I said. It's experience. If she's been a difficult baby so far, it's not because she has you pegged as a bad parent. You just don't know all the tricks yet. Besides, she's been through a lot in her short life."

Was it really that simple? Time would heal all wounds? Watching Peyton sleep on Jonathon's shoulder, Wendy certainly hoped so. But she couldn't help worrying if there was more to it than that. That there were deficiencies no amount of experience could compensate for. After all, she'd never be Peyton's real mother.

Almost as if he could read her mind, Jonathon added, "Give her some time. Give yourself some time too." Then Jonathon let out a bark of laughter. "Jeez, I sound like Dr. Phil."

She laughed along with him, despite the lump of sorrow burrowing into her chest. "Don't worry. I won't tell anyone at work."

"Thanks."

A moment of silence stretched between them. She should leave. Take advantage of Peyton's sleep to go shower or something. Yet she found her feet rooted to the ground as she watched him rocking the tiny infant.

"Why aren't you a father?" she asked, almost before she realized she meant to say it.

He arched an eyebrow.

Heat crept into her cheeks. "I mean, clearly you're great with kids. It seems like a no-brainer that you should have some of your own."

"I get frustrated enough trying to get Matt to clean up his third of the office."

"I'm serious."

"So am I. I've never had any desire to be a father." His tone was harsh, leaving no room for doubt. The touchy-feely portion of their discussion was over. "She should be asleep for a couple of hours at least. You should take advantage of it and get some breakfast."

"Thanks. I will."

She left the room without looking back, but with his words still echoing in her mind. He'd never wanted to be a father. Yet he'd just signed up for a two-year gig. She'd assumed when he asked her to marry him that he wouldn't be playing an active role in raising Peyton. But less than twenty-four hours in and he'd cared for Peyton more than she had.

He was going to an awful lot of trouble to keep her around. She could only hope she was half as good an assistant as he thought she was. Because she was certainly going to need to earn her keep.

Since he'd insisted repeatedly that he didn't need her, she wandered down to the kitchen for breakfast. She'd never even stepped into his house before last night. It wasn't quite what she'd expected. Like Matt, a few years before, Jonathon had bought one of the ridiculously expensive craftsman houses in Old Palo Alto. Though the homes were aging and modest, the neighborhood was one of the more expensive in the country. The interior of Jonathon's house had been renovated to its early-20th-century glory with meticulous detail. The furniture was a collection of authentic Mission antiques and clean-lined Japanese pieces that complemented them. She found the kitchen surprisingly well stocked. Not in the mood to cook anything, she rummaged through his pantry until she found a box of Pop-Tarts. She eyed them warily for a second—because Jonathon so did not seem like the Frosted Strawberry Pop-Tart type—then snagged a package and headed back upstairs.

She took a leisurely shower, nibbling on the pastry as she dressed. Jonathon had never been one of those men who didn't know how to ask for help. If he'd needed her before now, he would have woken her up. She'd gotten enough phone calls at six o'clock in the morning over the years to know that. Whatever he was doing with Peyton, he didn't need her immediately. Confident that Peyton must still be asleep, she took the time to linger over her grooming in a way she hadn't in the past couple of weeks. She did things like brush her hair. Floss her teeth. And put on ChapStick.

The rest had done wonders for her. Not only had she finally gotten a decent night's sleep, but obviously Jonathon had handled Peyton with perfect competence. Just as he'd said he would. That one small thing renewed her faith in this whole endeavor.

They had a week before they left for Texas. Which was more than enough time for them to settle into enough of a routine to fool her parents and family about their relationship. Jonathon obviously knew enough about babies that he'd be able to help her over the rough spots she was sure to encounter.

They'd spend a quick weekend in Texas convincing her family that they were Peyton's perfect guardians. Then they'd head back to Palo Alto and their lives would return to normal. Or as normal as they could be since she and Jonathon were now married and living together. All in all, life seemed damn good.

Once she'd verified that Peyton wasn't asleep in the nursery, she headed downstairs. She was about halfway down the stairs when she heard voices. Trepidation tripped along her nerves as she paused, head tilted to better hear the conversation coming from the kitchen.

Heart pounding, she made her way there. It could be Ford or Matt. Or a neighbor. Or… Then she heard it. Just outside the swinging door leading into the kitchen. A deep Texas twang.

"We would have come earlier if you'd given us more warning that y'all were fixin' to get married."

She squeezed her eyes closed, fighting back a burst of panic as she blew out a long breath. Then she shoved open the door and walked into the kitchen. To face her family.

Seven

Having lived his entire life in the northern half of California, Jonathon had weathered his share of earthquakes. He'd long ago gotten over whatever fear he might have had of them. But there were plenty of other act-of-God weather systems that scared the crap out of him. Tornadoes. Hurricanes. Tsunamis.

Anything that would swoop in and level an entire coastal plain deserved a healthy dose of respectful fear.

Clearly, Wendy's family fell into that category.

About ten minutes after Wendy had disappeared to take a shower, her family had arrived on his doorstep in a tidal wave of hearty handshakes, welcoming slaps and tearful hugs. It was a bit overwhelming, given that he'd never met any of them and would have had no idea who they were if he hadn't recognized her uncle, Big Hank, from the news clips he'd seen of the senator. And before Jonathon knew it, Wendy's parents, Tim and Marion, had swept into the house, followed by Big Hank, carefully lending an arm to the infamous Mema.

Jonathon had barely recovered from the stinging clap on the arm from Big Hank, when he faced down Mema. After Wendy's description, he'd half expected an old battleship of a woman. Instead, Mema was thin and stooped, fragile in appearance despite the strength of will that seemed to radiate from her.

A hush fell over the other members of the family as she shook his hand and appraised him. She had the wizened appearance of a woman who had lived hard and buried too many loved ones, but who was not yet ready to release her control over the rest of her clan.

She eyed him up and down. "Well, at least you're real."

"You doubted it?" he asked.

She sniffed indignantly. "I wouldn't put it past Gwen to invent a husband just to defy me."

"I assure you, ma'am. I'm real."

"As for what kind of father you'll be for my great-granddaughter, that we'll have to see about." Then her steely gaze narrowed with sharp perception and raked over Jonathon a second time. Finally she gave a little nod. "I've never had much use for overly handsome men. But then, neither has my Gwen, so I suppose there must be more to you than good looks."

He offered a wry smile. "I should hope so."

It was almost thirty minutes later when Wendy came down. The guarded look on her face as she walked through the door told him she'd heard them before entering the kitchen.

She was greeted with hugs that lasted longer and more joyful tears than he would have expected, given the way she'd described the strained relationship she shared with her family. Throughout it all, she kept a careful eye on Peyton, who was currently being held by Wendy's mother, as if Wendy expected that any moment the family might escape with the baby.

"What are y'all doing here?" she asked when she was finally able to get a word in edgewise.

He suppressed a smile. In five years, he'd never heard a hint of the Texas accent her family all sported. But three minutes in their company and she was slipping into *y'alls.*

"Oh, honey," her mother cooed, her voice all sugary sweet. "Of course we would come for your wedding. If we'd had enough warning, we would have been here." She shook her head, tears brimming in her eyes. "I can't believe I missed the wedding of my only daughter."

"I did tell you a week ago we were getting married. If you'd really wanted to come, you could have."

"But Big Hank had the jet in D.C.," her mother bemoaned, "and we had to wait until he could fit the trip into his schedule."

Jonathon felt a pang of regret, but Wendy muttered, "I'm glad to know you found the idea of flying commercial more repugnant than the prospect of missing my wedding."

Tim's head snapped up. "Young lady, you'll speak respectfully to your mother."

"Or what?" Wendy asked, anger creeping into her voice. "You'll cut off my allowance? The woman has missed almost every major event in my life since I was ten. And those that she showed up for, she criticized endlessly. I think she'll live."

"Gwen—" her mother started to protest.

Then Mema cleared her throat and both Wendy

and her mother fell silent. Their heads swiveled to face her.

"In the wake of our Bitsy's recent and tragic death, it is time for you to put aside your past differences." She stared them both down. Mother and daughter both dropped their gazes. "Now, the flight from Texas was long and I'd like to clean up before resting a bit before lunch." She turned to Jonathon. "I assume all the bedrooms are on the second floor?"

"They are," he said, not sure what she was getting at.

"Very well, then. I noticed an office just off the foyer. I'll sleep there. I don't do stairs well. Big Hank, please arrange for a bed to be delivered before evening. In the meantime, I'll rest on the sofa there."

Jonathon watched in amazement as a senior U.S. senator practically leaped to help his mother out of the kitchen. A moment later, Wendy's father had been sent out to the limo to instruct the driver where to bring the bags, and her mother had retreated to the nursery "to get reacquainted with her great-niece."

The second Jonathon and Wendy were all alone, she practically threw up her hands. "Why didn't you come get me the second they arrived?"

"You were dressing. I told them they could wait until you came down."

She tilted her head, studying him as if he were some foreign life form she'd never seen before. "You stood up to them?"

Ah. So that's what had her so puzzled. "Yes. I stood up to them. Do people not normally do that?"

She gave a bemused chuckle. "No. People don't normally do that." Shaking her head, she started carrying coffee cups from the kitchen table to the sink. Almost under her breath, she said, "I once dated a guy whose parents were lifelong members of Greenpeace. He'd spent every summer since he was ten on boats protesting whaling in Japan. He'd marched on Washington forty-four times before he was twenty. He'd been a vegan since he was three. Within thirty minutes of meeting my family, he was eating barbeque and smoking cigars out on the back porch with Big Hank." Shaking her head, she started rinsing out coffee cups and loading them into the dishwasher. "Within a week, he'd accepted a job working for my dad."

Jonathon studied the tense lines of her back. Her tone had been sad, but resigned. "The guy sounds like an idiot."

"No. He was very smart. The last I heard, Jed was VP of marketing for Morgan Oil. And Daddy would never promote anyone that high up who wasn't brilliant."

Jonathon gently turned her away from the sink and tipped her chin up to look at him. "That's not the kind of idiot I mean."

Her gaze met his, confusion in her eyes for a minute. Then her gaze cleared as she realized his meaning. Pink tinged her cheeks and pulled away from his touch. Tucking her hair back behind her ear she swallowed. "Thank you. For standing up to them, I mean. For everything."

"You're welcome."

She gave a bitter laugh. "You say that now. But you don't actually know what you've gotten yourself into." She looked pointedly at the kitchen door through which her family had left not long before. "This nonsense with them sweeping down on us unannounced? Inviting themselves to stay here? Ordering a bed for Mema to sleep on? This is all just the beginning. It'll only get worse."

"Of course it will," he stated as blandly as he could. "You think I didn't know that the second I opened the door?"

"I…I don't know. I guess… Most people don't see them for what they are."

"Try to have a little faith in me," he chided.

"I'm just warning you. My dad and Uncle Hank will woo you with their good ol' boy charm. And just when you think that you're their buddy and they're nothing more than simple roughnecks, they'll use that keen intelligence of theirs to manipulate you. And if they can't control you, they'll try to squash you."

"Consider me warned." He nodded. "Coming here was obviously a power play. They think they have the upper hand because they've chosen the time and location of the showdown. They're trying to establish themselves as the decision makers in the relationship. What about your mother? She seems harmless enough."

"Um, no." Wendy thought about it. Of all the family members, her relationship with her mother was the most complicated. There were times when she actually liked her mother. Of course, she loved all of them, but her mother she actually liked. But she'd never understood her. And her mother had her moments of being just as vicious as Uncle Hank. "In all those scuba-diving trips you take, you ever been in the water with a jellyfish?"

"Several times. They sting like hell."

"Exactly. They look delicate and frail, but they have more than enough defenses. That's my mother in a nutshell. She can play the victim, but she's as smart as—" That's when it hit her. "Oh, crap."

"What?"

"The bedroom!" She leaped to her feet and dashed for the stairs.

Jonathon snagged her arm on the way past. "What?"

She whispered, just in case anyone was close enough to hear, "The guest bedroom. Where I slept last night."

He continued to stare blankly at her. Seriously? Mr. Genius couldn't figure this out?

She lowered her voice to a hiss. "Last night. On our wedding night. I slept in the guest bedroom." She resisted the urge to bop him on the forehead. "And now my mother is upstairs with Peyton. And if she sees the guest bedroom, she'll realize we didn't sleep together last night."

This time, she didn't wait around to see if his sluggish brain had started working at normal speed. Instead, she pulled her arm from his hand and made a break for the stairs. He was hot on her heels as she took the stairs two at a time.

She stopped at the top, breathing rapidly through her mouth and she looked around for her parents. A long gallery hall ran from the top of the stairs to the guest room at the end. They'd have to pass the nursery to get there.

Crap, crap and double crap.

This was going to be tricky. She crept down the hall, praying that Jonathon would walk as softly. Or head back downstairs if he couldn't.

She tiptoed right up to the doorway and pressed herself against the wall, listening. She heard the faint, steady creak, creak of a rocking chair.

If her mom was sitting in the chair rocking Peyton, there was a good chance Wendy could sneak past to the guest bedroom, make the bed and sneak out with anyone being the wiser. Or more importantly, becoming suspicious.

Slinking past the door, she heard two things that would have stopped her in her tracks if she hadn't been in such a desperate hurry. The first was Jonathon's heavy footfall behind her. The next was her father's voice from within the nursery.

She glanced through the open door, but saw no one. Maybe they'd make it. But when she heard the rocking chair still, she grabbed Jonathon's hand and made a dash for it.

If her parents heard them and followed, she and Jonathon would never have time to actually make the bed. Certainly not neatly enough to put her father off the scent.

And this wasn't the day to leave up to fate.

Pulling Jonathon into the room after her, turning him so his back was to the door, she flashed him a wry smile. "Sorry about this."

"About what?"

She only had an instant to appreciate how charming he looked with that bemused expression on his face before she launched herself at him. They both tumbled backward onto the bed in a tangle of arms and legs. He might have gasped with surprise. She didn't have a chance to notice, as she pressed her mouth to his and kissed him.

The second Jonathon felt Wendy's mouth on his, he gave up trying to figure out what she was doing. She'd been babbling about the bedroom one minute and kissing him like a woman overwhelmed by desire the next. A smart man knew when to hold his questions for later.

Instead, he wrapped his hand around the back of her head and deepened the kiss. Her lips moved over his in sensual abandon, her tongue stroking against his in the kind of soul-deep kiss that made a man forget everything except the burning need to possess.

Desire pounded through him, heating his blood and tightening his groin. He fought against the desperate need to strip her naked and plow into her. A need that had been building within him for what seemed like years. Hell, probably had been years. As desperately as he wanted her, he didn't want this. This frantic, rapid rush of sex without fulfillment.

He wanted more. He wanted all of her.

Rolling her over onto her back, he took control of the kiss. Her hand had started pulling his shirt out from his waistband. If her hot little hand so much as touched his bare chest, he'd lose the last shreds of his control. So he grabbed both her hands in his and pulled them over her head, pinning them there. She let out a low groan, arching her back off the bed.

Yes. This was what he wanted: her, on the brink. As desperate and needy as he felt.

He slowed the kiss down, exploring every sweet corner of her mouth. Loving her sleepy flavor, the faint hint of coffee. The smooth heat of her tongue against his. Her hips bucked against his as she ground the vee between her legs against the length of his erection. Even through the multiple layers of her clothes, he could feel the heat of her.

But it wasn't enough. Merely kissing her would never be enough. Not when there was so much of her body left to explore. That silken shoulder that had been tempting him for so long. That tender swath of skin along her collarbone. The hollow at the base of her throat. The glimpse of her belly he sometimes saw when she rose up on her toes to get a fresh ream of printer paper.

His hand sought the hem of her shirt. He slipped his hand up to her rib cage, relishing how incredibly soft her skin was. He felt the edge of her bra and hesitated. He'd waited years to touch her naked skin. His hand damn near trembled at the prospect.

But was this really what he wanted? A quick grope in the guest bedroom when her family was just down the hall?

No, he wanted her naked. Laid out before him like a feast. He wanted hours. Days.

He wanted—

Jonathon's head jerked up as he pulled back from Wendy and sent her a piercing look.

Her family was just down the hall. What the hell had she been—

A sound came from the doorway. A man clearing his voice.

Jonathon whipped his head around and saw

Wendy's parents standing in the doorway. Her mom, a perfect, older version of Wendy, stood with her hands propped on her hips, but the teasing smile on her lips softened any reproach in her gaze. Wendy's father, on the other hand, looked ready to throttle him.

With good reason.

The man had just caught him groping his daughter like a desperate teenager.

Wendy's dad growled—actually growled—with displeasure and took a step toward him. Wendy's mother grabbed her husband by the arm. Though the petite woman couldn't possibly have had the strength to stop the man in his tracks, her touch still gave him pause.

"Wendy, your father and I will be waiting for you in the hall. Why don't you come out in a minute when you've had a chance to get yourselves…under control."

A moment later the guest bedroom door closed.

Jonathon rolled off Wendy, planted his feet firmly on the ground and dropped his head into his waiting hands.

What a mess.

Wendy's parents—waiting in the hall with her dad looking as if he wanted to chew his ass out—were the least of his worries. Whatever criticism they'd deliver he'd take.

None of it would come even close to the talking to he was going to give himself. He'd completely lost control. For several moments there, he'd forgotten where they were. Forgotten that she wasn't really his to take whenever he wanted. Forgotten that this was merely a sham.

Worse still, she hadn't. Clearly, she'd manipulated the situation—manipulated him—all so that her family wouldn't notice the fact that she'd obviously slept in the guest room. And it hadn't even occurred to him that that's what she had been doing.

He drew in several deep breaths, but barely felt calmer. The scent of her was heavy in the air, and with every breath she only seemed to fill more of the room, rather than less. That faint pepperminty smell that was uniquely her. His very hands seemed steeped in her.

He sat fully up, looking over his shoulder. She'd scrambled back into the corner of the bed, pressed against the headboard. She looked almost afraid of him. He didn't blame her. His control felt too shaky just now to offer her any reassurances.

She bit down on her lip as she tucked a strand of hair behind her ear. It was a ridiculous effort, fixing that one strand of hair when the rest were still so mussed.

"I—" she started to say, then cleared her throat. "Boy, that was close."

Not trusting himself to say anything just yet, he merely raised one eyebrow. Apparently she had no idea just how close that had been. Just how lucky she was that her parents had walked in, since he'd been about three minutes away from taking her right there.

"I—I'm sorry," she stammered. "I couldn't think of any other way to distract them from the bed."

He pushed himself to his feet. "I doubt your parents noticed the bed."

She scrambled up onto her knees. "No. I mean, that was the idea, right?"

He gave a tight little nod, hating her a little bit in that moment. Or at least hating that she was still thinking coherently when he'd lost the ability. "Yeah," he said as blandly as he could manage. "Apparently it was."

"I—" She climbed off the bed, coming to stand right beside him. "I'm sorry."

He was struck suddenly by how petite she was. Standing flat-footed beside him, the top of her head barely reached his chin. And yet, she never seemed small. She had more than enough personality to fill a woman half a foot taller. And more than enough strength of will to stand up to him.

He hadn't been able to face her father without embarrassing himself a few minutes ago, but her endless stream of excuses certainly killed the mood. She hadn't been as affected by the kiss as he had. Fine. But she could damn well stop harping on it.

"Stop apologizing," he ordered. "We all make mistakes. I'm just not used to making such stupid ones."

She opened her mouth as if to say something, but snapped it shut again when he brusquely smoothed down her hair. Then, since he couldn't seem to keep his hands off her, he pressed one quick kiss to her forehead. "Let's go face your parents."

Eight

Some things are embarrassing no matter what your age. Having your father stare down your boyfriend is one of them.

At seventeen, she and her boyfriend had been caught necking in the back of his truck. The make-out session had been bad enough. Worse still was the fact that her date had been high. Her father wasn't very forgiving of that sort of thing. Never mind that she hadn't known it at the time. She'd gotten reamed. He'd had the poor boy arrested. And had her hauled in and tested for drug use just to make a point. Was it any wonder the next year when she went to college she'd picked one thousands of miles away?

She'd always assumed that would be the low point

of her boyfriend/father debacles. But this—oddly enough—felt worse.

Maybe it was because Devin—or had it been Drake?—had been carefully chosen for his many red-flag qualities. He'd been guy number twenty-six in her ongoing teenage quest to piss off her parents.

As she followed Jonathon into the hall, she held her breath, half afraid of the argument to come and half relieved to be escaping Jonathon's one-on-one scrutiny.

Her parents were waiting for them in the hall. Her mother sent a wan smile, a hint of apology in her eyes. Her father, on the other hand, looked as if he could happily strangle Jonathon with his bare hands. Which was saying something, because Wendy had always figured it her father was going to murder someone, as a lifelong hunter and a member of the NRA, he would opt for a gun rather than sheer brute force.

Even with Devin—or was it Derek?—her father hadn't seemed this mad. Normally, she knew how to handle her parents. Twenty-three solid years of pushing their buttons made her an expert at undoing the damage. But just now, she was drawing a blank. Every brain cell she had was still stuttering with the memory of that soul-searing kiss.

He could have taken her right there, with her parents on the other side of the door, and she would have been okay with that. More than okay. She would have been begging for more.

Not a good thought, that one.

Since she could barely put a single coherent thought together, she was infinitely thankful that Jonathon seemed to be recovering more quickly than she was.

He draped an arm over her shoulder in a possessive, but nonsexual way. Giving her parents a distant nod, he said, "Mr. and Mrs. Morgan, I'm sorry you saw that."

"Oh, no need to apologize—" her mother began.

"You're sorry we *saw* that." Her father talked over her mother. "Or you're sorry you *did* it?" His tone was as ice-cold as his reproof. "Because to my way of thinking, a man who loves his wife doesn't fool around with her in the middle of the morning when her family is in the house and the child they hope to rear is in the next room."

"Dad!"

"Now, Tim—"

Jonathon held up a hand, stopping both her protest and her mother's. He drew out the moment just long enough for everyone to know he wasn't about to just kowtow to her father's bullying. "And to my way of thinking, a family that respects their daughter doesn't show up on her doorstep unannounced."

Her mother opened her mouth, looked ready to say something, then pressed her lips into a tight line and stomped off down the stairs.

Wendy's father continued to glare at Jonathon. Jonathon did a damn fine job of glaring back.

"If you think making my wife cry will endear you to me," her father said through gritted teeth, "then you're sorely mistaken."

Wendy wanted to protest. Those hadn't been tears in her mother's eyes. Just anger. But Jonathon didn't give her a chance to point it out.

"The same goes for you. Sir," Jonathon bit out. But apparently he couldn't leave well enough alone. Because a second later he stepped closer to her father and said, "And I'll have you know, that before she agreed to marry me, I never once so much as touched your daughter at work. I have the greatest respect for her intelligence. And her decisions. I'm not sure you can say the same."

Both men seemed to expand to fill their anger. Any second now, they would either start bumping their chests together like roosters or one of them would throw the first punch.

She figured they were equally matched. Her father was a solid six-five, and a barrel-chested two hundred and fifty pounds. Plus, he'd worked on rigs alongside roughnecks in his youth. Jonathon, on the other hand, had grown up poor, spent a few weeks in juvie, and had two older brothers, both of whom had criminal records. She figured he could probably handle himself.

She looked from one man to the other. Neither of them seemed to be willing to budge. Finally, she just shook her head. "I'm going to go talk to Mom. You two, sort this out." She gave Jonathon's arm a little squeeze, willing him to see her apology in her eyes. Then, as she walked passed her dad, she laid a hand on his arm. "Dad, I'm not seventeen anymore. And if Jonathon was planning on besmirching my honor or whatever it is you're worried about, then he probably wouldn't have married me. Give him a chance. You have no idea how good a guy he is."

She went down the stairs, half expecting her father and Jonathon to come tumbling down after her in a jumble of brawling arms and legs. And she tried to tell herself that if they did, it wasn't any of her business.

Peyton was apparently asleep again, because a stream of lullabies could be heard through the baby monitor sitting on the kitchen counter. Her mother was doing what most Texas women do when they're upset. Cooking.

Wendy gave a bark of disbelieving laughter.

Her mother's head jerked up, her eyes still sharp with annoyance. She had a hand towel slung over her shoulder, paring knife in her hand and a chicken defrosting in the prep sink.

She gave a sniff of disapproval before returning to the task at hand, dicing celery.

Wendy bumped her hip against the edge of the island that stretched the length of the kitchen. That honed black granite was like the river of difference that always divided them. Her mother on one side: cooking to suppress the emotions she couldn't voice. Wendy on the other: baffled at her mother's ability to soldier on in silence for so many years.

"You might as well just say it," her mother snapped without looking up from the celery.

"I didn't say anything," Wendy protested.

"But you were thinking it. You always did think louder than most people shout."

Wendy blew out a breath. "Fine. It's just..." Anything she said, her mother would take as a criticism. There was probably no way around that. "You're alone in the kitchen for less than five minutes and you start cooking?"

Her mother arched a disdainful brow. "Someone has to feed everyone. You know Mema isn't going to want to go out to eat. God only knows what the food is like up here."

Wendy laughed in disbelief. "Trust me. There are plenty of restaurants in Palo Alto that are just fine. Even by your standards. And we're a thirty-minute drive to San Francisco, where they have some of the best restaurants in the world. I think on the food front, we're okay. And if Mema doesn't want to go out, there are probably two dozen restaurants that would deliver."

Naturally, having food delivered wasn't something that would have occurred to her mother. Back in Texas, all of the Morgans lived within a few miles of each other, in various houses spread over the old Morgan homestead, deep in the big piney woods of East Texas. Sure you could have food catered out there, but not delivered. As a kid, Wendy used to bribe the pizza delivery guys with hundred-dollar tips, but that only worked on slow nights.

Her mom sighed. "I've already—"

"Right. You've already started defrosting the chicken." Here her mother was, making chicken and dumplings. Wendy could barely identify the fridge, given that it was paneled to match the cabinetry. She walked down the island, so she stood just opposite her mother. "Give me a knife and I'll get started on the carrots."

Her mother crossed to a drawer, pulled out a vegetable peeler and knife, then pulled a cutting board from a lower cabinet. A few seconds of silence later and Wendy was at work across from her mom.

Her mother had always been a curious mix of homespun Texas farmwife and old oil money. Wendy's maternal grandparents had been hardscrabble farmers before striking oil on their land in the sixties. Having lived through the dustbowl of the fifties, and despite marrying into a family of old money and big oil, her mother had never quite shaken off the farm dirt. It was one of the things Wendy loved best about her mom.

"You used to love to help me in the kitchen," her mother said suddenly.

Wendy couldn't tell if there was more than nostalgia in her voice. "You used to let me," she reminded her mother. She paused for a second, considering the carrot under her knife. "But you never really needed me there. I stopped wanting to help when I realized that whatever I did wasn't going to be good enough."

Her mother's hand stilled and she looked up. "Is that what you think?"

Wendy continued slicing the carrots for a few minutes in silence, enjoying the way the knife slid through the fibrous vegetable. As she chopped, she felt some of her anger dissipating. Maybe there was something to this cooking-when-you're-upset thing.

"Momma, nothing I've ever done has been good enough for this family." She gave a satisfying slice to a carrot. "Not my lack of interest in social climbing. Not my unfocused college education." She chopped another carrot to bits. "And certainly not my job at FMJ."

"Well," her mother said, wiping her hands on the towel. "Now that you've landed Jonathon—"

"No, Momma." Wendy slammed the knife down. "My job at FMJ had nothing to do with landing a husband. If all I wanted was a rich husband, you could have arranged that for me as soon as I was of age." Picking the knife back up, she sliced through a carrot with a smooth, even motion. Keep it smooth. Keep it calm. "I work at FMJ because it's a company I believe in. And because I enjoy my work. That's enough for me. And for once in my life, I'd like for it to be enough for you and Daddy."

"Honey, if it seems like I've been trying to fix you your entire life, it's because I know how hard it is to not quite fit in with this family. I know how hard this world of wealth and privilege can be to people who are different. I didn't want that for you."

"Momma, I'm never going to fit into this world. I'm just not. Your constant browbeating has never done anything except make me feel worse about it."

Her mother blanched and turned away to dab delicately at her eyes, all the while making unmistakable sniffling noises. "I had no idea."

Wendy had seen her mother bury emotions often enough to recognize this for the show it so obviously was.

"Oh, Momma." Wendy rolled her eyes. "Of course you did. You just figured you were stronger than I was and that eventually you'd win. You never counted on me being just as strong willed as you are."

After a few minutes of silence, she said softly, "I'm sorry, Mom."

Her mother didn't pretend to misunderstand. "Apology accepted."

"I really do wish you'd been here for the wedding. I guess I should have made sure you knew that."

Her mom slapped the knife down onto the counter. "You *guess?*"

"Yes," she said slowly, putting a little more force into the chopping. "I *guess* I should have."

"I am your mother. Is it so wrong for me to wish you'd wanted me here enough to—"

"Oh, this is so typical," she said. "Why should I have to beg you to come to my wedding? I've lived in California for over five years. When I first moved here, I invited y'all out to visit all the time. You never came. No one in the family has shown any interest in my life or my work until now. But now that baby Peyton is here, you've descended like a plague of locusts and—"

"My land," her mother said, cutting her off, her hands going to her hips. "And you wonder why we didn't want to come before now, when you talk about us like that."

Wendy just shook her head. Once again, she'd managed to offend and horrify her mother. Somehow, her mother always ended up as the bridge between Wendy and the rest of the Morgans. The mediator pulled in both directions, satisfying no one.

"Look, I didn't mean it like that. Obviously I don't think you're a locust. Or a plague."

"Well, then, how did you mean it?"

"It's just—" Bracing her hands on either side of the cutting board, she let her head drop while she collected her thoughts. She stared at the neat little carrot circles. They were nearly all uniform. Only a few slices stood out. The bits too bumpy or mis-shapen. The pieces that didn't fit.

All her life, she'd felt like that. The imperfect bit that no one wanted and no one knew what to do with. Until she'd gone to work for FMJ. And there, finally, she'd fit in.

Her mother just shook her head, sweeping up the pile of diced celery and dumping it in the pot. "You're always so eager to believe the worst of us."

"That's not true."

"It most certainly is. All your life, you've been rebellious just for the sake of rebellion. Every choice you've made since the day you turned fifteen has been designed to irritate your father and grand-mother. And now this."

"What's that supposed to mean?"

"Remember when you were fifteen and you and Bitsy bought those home-perm kits and gave yourselves home perms four days before picture day at the school?"

She did remember. Of course she did. Bitsy had ended up with nice, bouncy curls. But she'd been bald for months while her hair grew back out. Her father had been so mad his face had turned beet-red and her mother had run off to the bathroom for a dose of his blood-pressure medicine.

That had not been her finest moment.

"Or the time you wanted to go to Mexico with that boyfriend of yours. When we told you no, you went anyway."

"You didn't have to have the guy arrested," she said weakly. She couldn't muster any real indignation.

"And you should have told him you were only sixteen."

Also, not her proudest moment.

"And don't try to say we were being overprotective. No sane parent lets their sixteen-year-old daughter leave the country with a boy they barely know."

"Look, Mom, I'm sorry. I'm sorry I was such a difficult teenager. I'm sorry I never lived up to your expectations. But that has nothing to do with who I am now."

"Doesn't it?" Her mom swept up the carrots Wendy had been chopping and dumped them into the pot, lumpy, misshapen bits and all. She added a drizzle of oil in the pan and cranked up the heat. "You've rushed into this marriage with this man we've never even met—"

There was a note of censure in her voice that Wendy just couldn't let pass. "This man that I've worked with for years. If you've never met him, it's because you never came out to visit."

Her mother planted both her hands on the counter between them and leaned forward. "Jonathon seems like a very nice man. But if you married him solely to annoy us then—"

"Oh, Marian, don't be so suspicious."

Wendy spun around toward the kitchen door to see her father and Jonathon standing just inside. She and her mother had been so intent on their own conversation that neither of them had heard them enter.

The two men had obviously come to an understanding about the argument upstairs. Her father had his arm slung over Jonathon's shoulders as if they were old buddies. The smile on his face was downright smug.

Jonathon looked less comfortable. In fact, he rather looked like he'd swallowed something nasty.

Slowly his gaze shifted from her mother to her. Obviously, he heard everything her mother said to her. And he didn't like it.

Nine

"I'm sure," Wendy's father was saying, "that our little Gwen here has grown out of her rebellions."

Jonathon swallowed the tight knot of dread in his throat. "Mrs. Morgan, I assure you—"

But Wendy's mother sent both of them withering glares and he was smart enough to shut up when a woman wielding a butcher knife sent him a look like that.

Wendy pointed the tip of her own knife in her father's direction. "You stay out of this." For the first time in years she felt as though she and her mother were actually talking. She wasn't about to let her father muck it up.

Turning her gaze back to her mother, she continued as if the men hadn't entered at all. "I'm not a rebellious teenager anymore. I'm a grown woman. With a job I love. I may not have married the next political golden boy and I may not be VP of Twiddling My Thumbs at Morgan Oil, but I'm successful in my own right. And a lot of people would be proud to have me as their daughter."

"It's not that we're not proud," her mother began. "But—"

"Of course there's a but. There's always a but."

Her mother ignored her interruption, slicing to the point of the matter as easily as she sliced through the joints in the chicken. "But you've always delighted in rebelling against your father at every turn. If I thought for a minute that marrying Jonathon and raising Peyton was truly what you wanted—"

"It is."

"—and not just another one of your rebellions then I would support you wholeheartedly."

Wendy threw up her hands. "Then support me!"

"But I know how you are. If Mema or Big Hank, let alone your daddy, announced that the sky is blue, the very next morning you'd run out and join a research committee to scientifically prove that it's not."

"You make me sound completely illogical." Wendy

shook her head as if she didn't even know how to defend herself against her mother's accusations. "It's like you haven't heard anything I just said."

"Well, you tell me whether or not this is just rebellion." Her mom propped her fists on her hips. "Everyone in this family thinks Hank Jr. and Helen should raise Peyton, except you. Do you have any logical reason why you're so darned determined to raise this baby?"

Jonathon had had enough. He stepped away from her father. Pulling Wendy back against his chest, he said calmly, "I believe that's the point, isn't it? Everyone in the family except for Wendy. And Bitsy. Since Bitsy didn't want her brother raising her daughter, shouldn't that be enough for everyone?"

Marian snapped her mouth closed, narrowing her gaze and setting her jaw at a determined angle. He'd seen that look often enough on Wendy.

"You didn't know Bitsy," she said to him, obviously making an effort to moderate her tone. "Bitsy was never happy if she wasn't stirring up trouble. I don't like to speak ill of the dead, but has it occurred to either of you that naming Wendy guardian might just have been her way of creating conflict from beyond the grave?"

He felt Wendy pulling away from him, tensing to speak. He tugged her back soundly against him and said, "I may not have known Bitsy. But I know Wendy. I know she's going to make a wonderful mother."

Her mom studied him for a second, apparently searching for signs of his conviction. Finally, she nodded. "Hank Jr.'s wife, Helen, sees that baby as little more than a crawling, crying dollar sign. Peyton is a fast ticket to a bigger chunk of Mema's estate. Helen will fight you for that baby."

"Helen has three boys of her own that she's done a crappy job raising," Wendy pointed out. "If she hadn't shipped those boys off to boarding school the second they were old enough to go, maybe I'd see things differently."

"Just be prepared. Helen's like a bulldog with a bone when money's involved."

"That may be true," Jonathon said. "But Helen isn't here now. And we have all weekend to convince Mema that we'll be the best parents for Peyton."

Her mother harrumphed. "Don't think Helen hasn't figured that out as well. Mark my words, girly, you might be glad we came to visit you here instead of waiting for you to come to us. This might be your only chance alone with Mema to convince her that you and Jonathon are the happy, loving couple you want us all to believe."

There were few things that terrified Jonathon. He thought of himself as a reasonable and logical man. Irrational fears were for small children. Not adults.

At nineteen, he'd spent a solid hour in the dorm room of a buddy, holding the guy's pet tarantula in his hand to get himself over his fear of spiders. At twenty-three, about the time he'd made his first million, he'd spent three weeks in Australia learning how to scuba dive. That trip had served the joint purpose of getting him over his irrational fear of sharks and his equally irrational fear that FMJ would go under if he wasn't available 24/7.

He now took annual diving vacations. After the first, he'd stayed closer to home.

He was a man who faced his fears and conquered them.

Which didn't entirely explain why at nearly midnight on Saturday, he was still sitting in the kitchen sipping twenty-year-old scotch with Wendy's father and uncle. He'd been there for hours, listening to them tell stories about Texas politics and—as her father colorfully called it—"life in the oil patch."

Her family was entertaining, to say the least. And that was the sole reason he hadn't headed to bed much earlier. This had nothing to do with the fact that Wendy was now sleeping in his bed.

He'd been dreading sleeping in the same bed, but that was unavoidable now. As if that wasn't bad enough, now he couldn't get her mother's words out of his head.

After reminding Wendy over and over again that his own motives were selfish, why did it bother him to think that hers might not be so pure? He didn't know. All he knew was that he hated the idea that their marriage was just one more rebellion in a long line of self-destructive behaviors. Worse still was the idea that she'd quickly lose interest in him once the tactic failed to shock her parents.

If she offered herself to him, he wouldn't be able to resist. Even knowing what he did now, the temptation would be too sweet.

To his chagrin, he actually felt a spike of panic when her uncle stood, tossed back the last of his drink and said, "Jonathon, I appreciate the hospitality—and the scotch—but I know I'll regret it tomorrow if I drink any more."

Wendy's dad stood as well. "Marian is gonna have my hide tomorrow as it is."

Jonathon held up the decanter toward Wendy's father. "Are you sure I can't offer you another?"

"Well..."

But Hank slapped his brother on the arm in a jovial way. "We're keeping him from his bride."

"Don't remind me," her father grumbled.

"No man should have to entertain a couple of old blowhards when he has a lovely new wife to warm his bed."

Jonathon nearly smiled at that, despite himself. He liked Wendy's family far more than he wanted to admit. He knew she found them overbearing and pretentious, but there was something about their combination of good-ol'-boy charm and keen intelligence that appealed to him.

Besides, the longer he kept them here, shooting bull until all hours of the night, the greater the chance that Wendy would be fast asleep by the time he got up to the bedroom.

However, before he could even offer them yet another drink, Wendy's father and uncle were stumbling arm in arm up the stairs to the guest bedrooms where they were staying. He winced as they banged into the antique sideboard his decorator had foolishly put outside his office. And then cringed as her father cursed loudly at the thing. Maybe he should consider himself lucky that all of their fumbling didn't wake Mema.

He waited until they vanished down the upstairs hall before he followed, turning off lights as he went. That afternoon, he and Wendy's father had moved Peyton's crib from the nursery to the master bedroom. Ironic, since it had only just arrived in the past week. They'd moved the spare mattress up from the garage and now the guest-bedroom-turned-nursery was once again a guest bedroom. Throughout the process, Wendy kept insisting that her family should just book rooms at one of the many hotels in town. Mema had looked scandalized. Marian had looked offended. And Wendy had eventually caved.

And so, after thirteen years of living completely by himself, he now had six additional people under the roof. Maybe he should buy a bigger house. One with more bedrooms. Though a dozen bedrooms wouldn't have saved him from this. When the family of your new wife was visiting, they all expected you to share a room with her. There was just no way around that.

After putting it off as long as he could, he finally bit the bullet and let himself into the master bedroom. The room he'd be sharing with Wendy. His wife.

Despite his numerous prayers, she wasn't asleep.

She sat up in the bed, her back propped against the enormous square pillows his decorator had purchased—personally he'd never been able to stand the damn things and wasn't entirely sure why he continued to pile them on the bed every morning.

Peyton was asleep on Wendy's chest, her tiny fist curled near her face so that she sucked on one knuckle. Wendy was on his side of the bed. The bedside lamp was on and in her other hand, she held a Kindle.

He glanced at the bedside table. Scratch that, she held his Kindle.

She looked up as he closed the door behind him. Try as he might, he couldn't force himself to walk into the room more than a step or two.

Wendy smiled sheepishly. "Sorry to steal your Kindle," she whispered. "She fell asleep here and I didn't want to risk waking her by digging around for my own book."

She was dressed in a white tank top and Teenage Mutant Ninja Turtle boxer shorts. Her legs were stretched out in front of her. How a woman as short as she was had ended up with legs that long was a mystery, but damn, they seemed to stretch for miles.

Her skin was creamy white, her legs lightly muscled, ending in perfect, petite feet. And her toenails were painted a sassy iridescent purple. He had to force his attention away from her bare legs, but couldn't make his gaze move all the way up to her face. He got caught on her arms, which were just as bare as her legs and somehow nearly as erotic.

In all those years that they'd worked together, he hadn't ever seen her in something sleeveless. Her upper arms were just like the rest of her. Small and lean, but lightly muscled. Unexpectedly strong.

There was something so intimate about the sight of her holding Peyton on her chest, dressed for bed. In *his* bed.

His muscles practically twitched with the need to cross the room and pull her into his arms. To do all kinds of wicked things to her body. Or maybe to just sit on the bed next to her and watch her sleep.

That thought—the idea that he'd be content without even touching her—that was the thought that scared the crap out of him. Physically wanting her, he could handle that. He'd been fighting his desire for her for years. He always won that battle. But this new urge to just be with her. He didn't even want to know what the hell that was about.

Suddenly his master bedroom seemed way too small.

That new house he was going to buy—the one

with a dozen guest bedrooms—apparently the master would need to be four times bigger. He was going to have to move out to Portola Valley to find a house big enough.

"You're mad, aren't you?" Wendy asked.

He dragged his gaze up to her face. She was frowning in that cute way she did, biting down on her lower lip in a half frown, half sheepish grin. He walked closer so that he didn't have to speak louder than a whisper. "Why?" he asked.

"You're mad that I borrowed your Kindle." She flicked the button on the side to turn it off. "I didn't even think. That was a horrible invasion of your privacy."

He wanted to stand here watching her sleep and she was worried that reading from his Kindle was an invasion of his privacy. She had no idea.

"It's okay. No big deal."

"Are you sure?" Despite the whisper, her voice sounded high and nervous. "Because you look really annoyed."

If anything, he probably looked as though he was trying not to kiss her. Good to know she interpreted that as annoyed. "It's just a Kindle. Not a big deal."

Then he crossed automatically to his side of the

bed. The side she was sitting on. He took off his watch and set it on the valet tray on the bedside table. The familiarity of the action calmed his nerves. Of course, normally there wasn't an empty baby bottle beside the lamp, but still…

"Did you have trouble getting her to fall sleep?" he asked as he pulled off his college ring and dropped it beside the watch. Then he hesitated at the simple gold band on his left hand. Since he'd slept in Peyton's nursery last night, he'd had both rings and the watch on all night. This was the first time he'd taken off the wedding ring.

"No." Wendy rubbed at her eyes a little before arching her back into a stretch. "I think she's finally getting used to the new feeding schedule. I woke her at eleven for that bottle and she went right back to sleep…."

Jonathon looked up when he heard her voice trail off. Like him, she was staring at the ring on his hand. Her gaze darted to his and held it for a second. He watched, entranced, as she nervously licked her lips. Something hot and unspoken passed between them, once again stirring that need to kiss her. To mark her as his own. To bend her back over the bed and plow into her.

Thank God, Peyton was asleep on her chest, keeping him from doing anything too stupid.

He yanked the ring off his finger and dropped it onto the tray beside his watch and his class ring.

Her gaze dropped to where his watch and rings lay on the nightstand. Then it snapped up to his face again. She gave another one of those wobbly, anxious smiles. "I'm on your side of the bed, aren't I?"

"It's fine."

"No, I'll move. Just give me a second." Bracing an arm at Peyton's back, she half sat up, then hesitated. Peyton squirmed and Wendy's frown deepened.

"Just lie her down in the center. She can sleep there."

"You sure?"

"Absolutely." Was it wrong that he was scheming to get Peyton in the bed between them? A little devious maybe, but not wrong. He wouldn't make a move on Wendy as long as Peyton was in the same room. But having her in the bed was a stroke of genius. Better than an icy shower, he was sure. And less conspicuous. Besides, he even had sound scientific reasoning in his corner. "I've been reading this book on—"

"Attachment parenting?" she asked as she waggled the Kindle. "I've been stalking your Kindle, remember?"

That playful, suggestive tone of hers was like a kick in the gut. Maybe he'd still need that cold shower. "I should just sleep on the floor."

"Don't be ridiculous."

She leaned over and rolled Peyton from her chest to the center of the bed. Then came up onto her hands and knees to climb over the still sleeping baby. The thin cotton of her boxer shorts clung enticingly to her bottom and his groin tightened in response to the sight.

She had no idea just how far from ridiculous he was being. This was him at his most practical.

Hell, forget the floor. He'd just sleep in the shower. With the cold water on.

"I don't mind."

"Well, I do," she said, tossing the pillows on that side of the bed onto the floor—the side that from this moment on would always be *her* side of the bed. "When I think of all the things you've done for me in the past few weeks…"

"Don't make me into some kind of hero. You know why I married you." The problem was he was no longer sure *he* knew why he'd done it. "My motives weren't altruistic."

At least that was true.

She flashed him a smile that was a little bit sad. "I know. But neither are mine. And I'm not about to kick you out of bed."

Ten

"Not about to kick you out of your *own* bed," she corrected, a blush tinting her cheeks.

As if she wasn't irresistible already.

He wanted to argue about the sleeping arrangements. Dear God, he did. But he couldn't logically make an argument for sleeping in the tub. Besides, he'd doubt he'd fit.

"Oh, I get it," she said with teasing concern. "You're embarrassed about your body."

Clearly she was trying to hide her own embarrassment. "Wendy—"

"You're probably all pasty white under those dress shirts, huh?" She clucked her tongue in sympathy. "Maybe you put on a few extra pounds over the holidays? Is that it? Is that why you're standing there like a statue, refusing to get undressed?"

He wasn't about to tell why he really wasn't getting undressed. If she hadn't figured out how thin her tank top was and how much that turned him on, then he wasn't going to be the one to tell her.

"Hey, I won't even look," she teased, making a great show of rolling over to face the wall. "Now I can't see you. You can even turn out the light if you want."

Rolling his eyes at her silliness, he reached over and turned off the lamp before starting on his buttons.

"I guess you made peace with my dad," she said after a minute.

"I guess so," he admitted, slipping off his shirt and tossing it vaguely in the direction of a nearby chair. He toed off his shoes and socks. "He's not such a bad guy."

"No." Her voice was small in the darkness. "He's not. Everyone comes around eventually."

He hesitated before unbuttoning his jeans. He hadn't slept in anything other than his underwear since college. He didn't even own a pair of pajama bottoms. First thing in the morning, he was buying a pair. No, twenty pair. Maybe thirty just to be safe.

A moment later he lay down so close to the edge of the bed that his left shoulder hung off the side. His awkward position was still not uncomfortable enough to block out the scent of her on his pillow. It smelled warm and feminine and faintly of peppermint.

He lay there stiffly, eyes resolutely closed, keenly aware that she too was still awake. He searched for something to say. "I never knew you liked the Teenage Mutant Ninja Turtles."

Damn, was he smooth or what?

He heard her roll over in the dark and prop herself up on her elbow. "Doesn't everyone?"

He turned just his head to look at her, but found himself eye to eye with Peyton. Her tiny face was seven inches from his. Her lips pursed as she dreamed about eating. He remembered his niece doing that, from all those long years ago when he used to help feed his sister's kids. Lacey would be in college now. He felt a powerful punch of longing. The kind he normally kept buried deep inside. To push it back down, he rolled up onto his elbow to look at Wendy.

At least he understood the longing he felt when he looked at her. Pure sexual desire. He got that. He could control it—at least, he thought he could. God knew, he'd controlled it so far. But this unfamiliar longing to reconnect with his family? That was new and terrifying territory.

He doubled his pillow under his head, allowing him to look over Peyton to where Wendy lay. She'd moved the night-light in from the nursery, a glowing hippo that cast the room in pink light and made Wendy's skin look nearly iridescent. When he looked back up at her eyes, her gaze darted away from his, as if she was all too aware of the desire pulsing through his veins.

He could see she was about to lie back down, so he said, "No, not everyone loves Teenage Mutant Ninja Turtles. Most people don't even know they were a witty and subversive comic book before becoming a fairly cheesy movie marketed to kids."

She gave a playful shrug, smiling, either because the topic amused her or because she was relieved he'd stopped looking at her like something he wanted to lick clean, he couldn't tell which.

"That's me, I guess." She imitated his hushed tone, obviously no more willing to wake Peyton than he was. "A fan of things witty and subversive."

"Yeah, I get that. What I don't get is how I never knew it until now."

"Oh." She gave another shrug, this one self-effacing.

"For five years, you've dressed like the consummate, bland executive assistant." Whispering in the dark as if this made the conversation far more intimate than the topic was. "Bland clothing in a neutral palate. Demure hair. Now I find out you've been hiding a love of violet nail polish and eighties indie punk rock." He nodded toward her boxers. "Not to mention the Turtles."

She frowned. "Punk rock?"

"The Replacements T-shirt you had on the other day."

"You recognized them?" She gave him a pointed once-over. "And yet you don't seem like a fan of eighties alternative."

"I'm a fan of Google. And you couldn't possibly have been old enough to attend the concert where that T-shirt was sold."

"I'm a fan of eBay. And of defying expectations."

"Which brings me back to my original question. Why didn't I know this about you?"

She paused, seeming to consider the question for a long time. Then she sank back and stared at the ceiling. He watched her, lying there with her eyes open as she gazed into the dark, long enough that he thought she wasn't going to answer at all.

Finally she said softly, "Working at FMJ…" Her

shoulders gave a twitch, as if she was shrugging off her pensive mood. "I guess it's been the ultimate rebellion for me. When you're from an old oil family, what's worse than working for a company that's made their money in green energy."

"We do a lot of other things too," he pointed out.

"Well, sure." She rolled back to face him. "But even then, it's all about innovation and change. My family is all about tradition. Maybe when I was working for FMJ, I never felt like I needed to rebel."

He felt his heart stutter as he heard her slip. *When I was working for FMJ,* she'd said. Not *now that I am working for FMJ,* but *when I was.* But she didn't seem to notice, so he let it pass without comment.

"Working at FMJ," she continued, her voice almost dreamy, "I felt like I had direction. Purpose. I didn't need to define myself by dying my hair blue or getting my navel pierced or getting a tattoo."

The image of her naked belly flashed through his mind. The thought of a tiny diamond belly-button ring took his mind into dangerous territory.

"A tattoo?" He was immediately sorry he asked. Please let it be somewhere completely innocuous, like her...nope. He couldn't think of a single body part on Wendy that didn't seem sexy.

She gave a little chuckle. "One of my more painful rebellions." Then—please God, strike him dead now—she lifted the hem of her white tank top to reveal her hip and the delicate flower that bloomed there.

He clenched his fist to keep from reaching out to touch it. For a second, every synapse in his brain stopped firing. Thought was impossible. Then they all fired at once. A thousand comments went through his brain. Finally, he cleared his throat and forced out the most innocent of them. "That doesn't look like it was done in a parlor."

As lovely as it was, the lines were not crisp. The colors weren't bright.

Wendy chuckled. "Mine was done by a boyfriend." She held up her hands as if to ward off his criticism. "Don't worry, his tools were all scrupulously sterilized and I've been tested since then for all the nasty things you can get if they hadn't been." She gave the tattoo a little pat and then tugged her hem back down. "I was eighteen, had just finished my freshman year at Dartmouth and I wanted to study abroad. My parents refused and made me come home and intern at Morgan Oil. So I dated a former gang member who'd served time in county."

Jonathon had to swallow back the shot of fear that jumped through his veins. She'd obviously survived. She was here now, healthy and safe, but the thought of her dating that guy made his blood boil.

He unclenched his jaw long enough to say, "And you wonder why your parents worry about you."

She gave a nervous chuckle. "Joe was actually a really nice guy. Besides, after spending the weekend with my family—"

"Let me guess, now he works for Morgan Oil? Interns for your uncle in Washington?"

"No. Even better. He went on to write a book about how to leave the gang life behind. He teaches gang intervention throughout Houston and travels all over the U.S. working with police departments."

"You sound almost proud," he commented.

She cocked her head and seemed to think about it. "I guess I am proud of Joe. He turned his life around." Then she gave a little laugh. "Maybe my family should start a self-help program."

"Tell me something. What's with all the cautionary tales?"

"What do you mean?"

"This is the second boyfriend you've told me about whose life was changed by meeting your parents."

"I'm just warning you." Her tone was suddenly serious. "This is what they do. They'll find your weakness—or your strength or whatever—and they use it to drive you away from me."

"No," he said. "That's what they've done in the past. That's not what they're going to do to me."

"Don't be so sure of that." She looked at him, her expression resigned. "Can you honestly tell me you haven't considered how helpful my uncle could be in securing that government contract?"

"That contract has nothing to do with this."

"Not yet. But they're doing it already."

"I don't—"

"You were up late drinking scotch with my dad and uncle, weren't you?"

"How—"

"I can smell it on your breath. And you don't drink scotch."

"How do you know that I don't drink scotch?"

"You never drink hard liquor." Her tone had grown distant. "Never. You keep very expensive brands on hand at the office—and I assume here—for associates who do drink. You read *Wine Spectator* magazine, and can always order a fabulous bottle of wine.

You don't mind reds and will drink white, if that's what your companion is having, but you don't really like either. You prefer ice-cold beer. Even then, you never have more than two a night."

He leaned back slightly, unnerved that she knew so much about his taste. "What else do you know about me?"

"I know that anyone who has such strict rules for themselves about alcohol, probably has a parent who drinks. I'd guess your father—"

"It was my mother."

"—but that would just be a guess."

"You have any other theories?"

Between them Peyton stirred. He reached out a hand to place on Peyton's belly to calm her. Wendy reached out at the same time and their fingers brushed. Wendy hesitated, then linked her fingers through his.

"I didn't say it to make a point. I'm just…" She brushed her thumb back and forth over his. "There's something about my family that makes people want to impress them. It's made you want to impress them, or you wouldn't have bent your no-hard-liquor rule."

"My mom did drink," he said slowly. "'Functioning alcoholic' is the term people use now. You have any other old wounds you want to poke?"

The second the words left his mouth, he squeezed his eyes shut.

Christ, he sounded like a jerk.

He opened his eyes, shoving up on his elbow to look at her. He fully expected to see a stung expression on her face. Instead, she just gave his hand a squeeze and sent him a sad smile.

"I'm sorry," he admitted.

"Don't apologize. I got a little carried away with the armchair psychology." She was silent for a minute and he could hear the gears in her brain turning. "But since you mentioned it…"

"Okay, hit me with it. What horribly invasive question are you going to ask next? You want to know my deepest fear? Clowns. How much I'm actually worth? About—"

"Actually I wanted to know about Kristi."

He fell silent.

"She was your—"

"I know who you mean."

He didn't say anything for a long time, all but praying she'd let it drop. She shifted in the bed beside him. Fidgeting, but saying nothing. She wasn't going to let it drop, and if he didn't respond soon, she'd think Kristi was a bigger deal than she had been.

"She was just someone I knew in high school. Who told you about her?"

He wanted to know who to kill. He hoped it wasn't Matt or Ford, because murdering one of his business partners would probably be the end of FMJ.

"Claire," Wendy answered.

Well, crap. He couldn't very well kill a woman. Especially when she'd just married his best friend.

"Don't be mad at her," Wendy continued. "I practically begged for information."

"Why on earth would you beg for information about my old high school girlfriend?"

"I dunno." She rolled over, but with his eyes squeezed shut, he couldn't tell if she was rolling toward him or away from him. "As dead set as you are against love…well, no one feels that way unless they've been hurt."

"What did Claire tell you about Kristi?"

She didn't answer right away. "Just that you were crazy about her. And she left."

She'd paused long enough for him to know she'd been fabricating her answer. Condensing it down to the barest details.

But in his mind, he could all too easily imagine the longer version. The real version. The one where he made a complete ass of himself over Kristi. Where he handed her his whole heart…and did nothing but scare her away.

"And?" he prodded.

"I figured…she must have been the one."

"And that's what you surmised from Claire's story? That Kristi was the one to break my heart?"

"Am I wrong?"

What exactly was he supposed to say to that? Kristi *had* broken his heart. But he'd only been eighteen. "That was a lifetime ago."

"What happened with her? What really happened?"

He forced his eyes open and tried to sound casual. "You're the armchair psychologist. What do you think happened?"

She tilted her head to the side, considering. "I think that you, Jonathon Bagdon, are a pretty intense guy."

He looked up at her. In the dark of the room, her skin was luminous. Her eyes were so dark they looked almost purple. She was so beautiful, it made his heart ache. As well as plenty of other parts of him.

Damn, but he wanted her. Not just her body. But all of her.

Thinking of her comment, all he could was mutter, "You have no idea."

"The way I see it, I'm a grown woman. Someone who's used to dealing with strong personalities. And there are times when even I'm a little overwhelmed by you. So this girl—Kristi?—she probably didn't have a chance. I'm guessing you falling in love with her must have scared the hell out of her."

"Yeah. That's about it." He let his eyes drift closed again. "This thing between us," he began, but then corrected himself, "this physical thing between us, it's pretty intense."

"Yes, it is," she agreed softly. He opened his eyes to see her still sitting up, looking down at him. The look in her eyes made heat churn through his body, but it was her words that made his heart pound. "I'm not scared of you, Jonathon."

"Maybe you should be."

She tilted her head, studying him in the pink glow of the hippo. Indeed, she looked more aroused than frightened. "Maybe."

"Scratch that. You should definitely be afraid. If you knew half the things I want to do to you…"

She arched a brow, her expression a little curious,

a little challenging. "You think you're the only one with pent-up desire and an active imagination?"

Was she purposefully trying to destroy any chance he had of getting some sleep? Ever again?

"I think," he answered her, "there's a damn good chance you underestimate how sexy you look in a tank top." It was hard to tell in the pink light, but he could have sworn she blushed. He couldn't stop himself from going on. "And I also think you underestimate just how hard it is for me to keep my hands off you."

Her chest rose as she sucked in a deep breath, highlighting all the wonderful things that tank top of hers did.

"You think you're the only person this is hard for?" she asked.

"I think I'm the only one who's a big enough jerk to wait until there was an innocent baby here in the bed between us, just to guarantee I'd keep my hands off you."

She gnawed on her lip for a second then, looking secretly pleased with herself. He squeezed his eyes shut, blocking out the image of her and that sexy bow mouth of hers.

He felt the bed shift as she lay back down. Then, so softly he thought he might have imagined it, she said, "Don't be so sure about that."

Eleven

She'd fallen asleep with her body fairly throbbing with unfulfilled sexual tension and she woke up alone. The feeling of jittery anticipation stayed with her as she headed for the bathroom and dug through the suitcases she'd left in Jonathon's closet the day before. She quickly pulled on an oversize gossamer shirt and a pair of black leggings and headed downstairs to search out food and her family.

She walked into the kitchen just in time for her mother to pile her plate high with the last batch of buttermilk pancakes. Peyton was gurgling happily in the high chair beside the table, being cooed to by Mema. The kitchen was as warm and as welcoming as a Hallmark special. The tangy scent of pancakes mingled with the bitter zing of the coffee to stir long-forgotten memories of her childhood. She swallowed back a pang of loneliness and regret. She'd chosen to leave Texas and to distance herself from her family. That didn't mean she didn't miss them.

But with all that was going on in the kitchen, there was one thing that was missing. Jonathon.

Or to be more precise, three things: Jonathon, her father and Big Hank.

She didn't notice at first, so caught up as she was in the pancake-scented time machine. But she paused, that first bite halfway to her mouth, and listened with her head cocked toward the kitchen door, mentally reviewing the walk down the stairs.

She set down the fork, heavenly bite uneaten. "Okay, where'd you send them?"

Mema's back stiffened. "Why would you assume I'd sent them anywhere?"

Wendy shoved the bite of pancakes into her mouth and chewed out her frustration. "Well, they're not here, are they? That means you've sent them off somewhere. Either so you can ply him for information. Or me, I suppose."

Her mother and grandmother exchanged a look that made her very nervous. She forked off another bite and crammed it in. Weren't carbs supposed to be calming? So why didn't she feel any more relaxed?

She felt a niggling of fear creep up her spine. If she was honest with herself, she knew why she didn't feel any calmer. When a pride of lions went hunting, they'd separate the weaker members of the pack from the rest to make it easier to pick them off.

Jonathon had just been separated from the herd.

"Where did they go?" she asked, feigning a calmness the pancakes hadn't provided.

"Seriously, it's nothing nefarious. Jonathon offered to show them FMJ's headquarters. It's not like they've taken him out back to beat him or anything."

No. Maybe it wasn't like that. But she feared how buddy-buddy they'd be when they got back.

She and Jonathon had only been married for two days and already her family was driving a wedge between them.

It was no easy task slipping out of the house when her mother and grandmother were there hovering. In the end, she lied. She wasn't proud of it, but she did it.

I just want to run out to the grocery store for a few things, she'd said. *Diapers. New formula. Oh, right.*

There are several cans in the pantry. But Peyton's been so fussy I want to try a different brand.

Who knew motherhood would provide such ample opportunity for lying?

"I think between the two of us, Mema and I have raised enough children to muddle through," her mother had said as Wendy headed for the door.

Wendy took the grocery store at a mad dash, storming the unfamiliar baby aisle as if it were the target of a shock-and-awe military campaign. She raked into her cart five different varieties of formula and enough diapers to keep Peyton dry until college. Then, back in the car, she retraced her path, bypassing Jonathon's street and heading for FMJ's headquarters.

Stopped at a light—mentally urging it to change more quickly—she took one brief minute to question her motives. Why was she so worried? What was the worst that would happen?

A few hours alone with her family wouldn't convince Jonathon to revamp his entire life, write a tell-all and travel the country on the lecture circuit. After a single night of tossing back scotch with her uncle, he wasn't going to quit FMJ and accept a position at Morgan Oil. Or worse, run for office.

But none of that logic slowed the pounding of her heart. Nor did it dry out her damp palms.

She so desperately wanted to believe that Jonathon was different than every other guy she'd ever dated. But what if he wasn't?

He had to know how influential her uncle was within the government. One word from Big Hank and that contract they'd been working on could be a done deal. All Jonathon had to do was sell her uncle on the idea.

And when it came to FMJ's proprietary technology, no one was a better salesman than Jonathon. If he had the chance to schmooze her uncle, he'd be a fool not to take it. She'd just hoped he wouldn't have a chance.

By the time she swiped her security card at the campus gate, she was twitchy with anxiety. Part of her wanted to just drive. Not back to his house, not even back to hers, but just drive. She'd had a friend once who hopped in her car and drove to Cabo San Lucas every time life got messy. It was a twenty-eight-hour drive from Palo Alto. By tomorrow afternoon, Wendy could be sipping tequila on the beach. But none of her problems would go away. And then she'd be drunk or hungover and two thousand miles from them. That hardly seemed like the perfect solution. Twenty-seven years of rational decision-making wouldn't let her go the Shawshank route.

She scurried into the front office, dropped her purse on the desk and sank into her chair. The simple familiarity of the actions settled her nerves. How crazy was it that the faint scent of ozone coming off all the computer equipment in the other room could be so calming?

Maybe her family was right and she was a nut for loving this job so much, but she couldn't help it. Everything felt right in the world when she sat behind this desk.

She knew it was an illusion. If she went down to the R&D lab, she'd find Jonathon there with her father and uncle. And she just wasn't ready to see that yet. Apparently, she'd run across town for nothing.

Letting out a sigh, she crossed her arms on the desktop and dropped her head into the cradle of her elbows. Then she heard a faint sound coming from the back office that Ford, Matt and Jonathon shared. She stilled instantly, listening. Slowly she stood and crossed to the door, giving it a nudge so it swung inward.

Jonathon stood behind his desk along the west wall. She was unused to seeing him in casual clothes, and couldn't help admiring how good he looked in a simple cotton T-shirt and jeans. Though his laptop was out on his desk, it wasn't open. There was a manila file in his hand.

"Oh," she murmured as he looked up. "It's you."

His lips twitched. "Who'd you expect?"

"I..." She paused, momentarily stumped. Finally, she admitted, "I thought you were downstairs in the R&D lab. With my father and Big Hank."

"Nope." He frowned, obviously puzzling through why she would have thought that. "We ran into Matt. He offered to show them around."

"Oh." Relief flooded her. He wasn't off schmoozing her family. He hadn't fallen under their spell.

"Why'd you come in?" he asked.

"Oh, well I..." Not wanting to admit she suspected him of underhanded business tactics, she made a vague gesture toward her office. "Same as you. Wanted to catch up on some work."

Suddenly, now that her fears about Jonathon had been dispelled, another emotion came rushing into the void left by them: desire. Or maybe it had been there all along, right under the surface, waiting for an excuse to rise to the top, as it always did.

"Right." He nodded. "Since I figure we won't be in tomorrow we might as well—"

"Why won't you be in tomorrow?" she asked, without really listening for the answer, because her mind was back in the bedroom, the night before, hearing him confess how much he wanted her. And she was remembering how he'd looked in the light of that ridiculous pink hippo, the bedsheet pulled only to his waist, the muscles of his chest so clearly defined despite the dim lighting.

"Your family. They'll still be here then."

"So? What does that have to do with your work?"

"While they're here, our first priority is convincing them we're a happy couple. We can't do that if we're not together."

"But work—" she protested.

"Can wait for a few days."

Work? Wait? Who was this guy?

Whoever he was, she didn't like it. Not one bit. She was going to have a hard enough time sleeping in the same bed with him for the next week. She'd been counting on their time at the office to return to normalcy. Now more than ever, she needed him to be the hard, analytical boss she was used to.

Her mind was still reeling from that little bomb when Jonathon said, "Since we're both here, why don't you go grab your computer and we'll try to get some work done?"

"The thing is, Jonathon, I—"

Then she broke off abruptly. Because what could she really say? He was waiting, expectantly. Looking so handsome it made her heart ache. "The thing is, I don't know if I can do this."

"Do what?"

"Slip so easily between the work me and the me that has to pretend to be your wife. I don't know why it seems so easy for you, but—"

"You think this is easy for me?"

"Well. Yes. You barely seem aware that at this time yesterday you were kissing me. Or that last night we slept in the same bed." She paused, waiting for him to say something. Though his gaze darkened, he didn't comment and suddenly she felt ridiculous for saying these things aloud. "Which is fine, I mean, this is my problem. I'll figure it out. But I think I just need to get out of here for a couple of hours. Get my head on straight."

Maybe that trip to Cabo wasn't such a bad idea after all.

She turned and had made it most of the way to the door when he grabbed her arm and turned her around. She barely caught her balance when he pulled her roughly against him and kissed her.

Twelve

His mouth was hot and firm on hers. It only took a second for her to lose herself in the sensation of being kissed by him. No, not just kissed, devoured. She felt completely swept away by it. By him. By the sensation of his hand gently cupping her jaw. By his arm at her back, pressing her body to his. The feel of his lips as they moved over hers in a hundred delicate kisses.

"This is not easy," he pulled back just long enough to say. And then he kissed her again. "It's never been easy." Another kiss. "Not once in five years." And another kiss. "Not once has it been easy." And another. "To stay away from you."

And then his tongue was in her mouth, seducing her with long, slow strokes, stirring heat in her body. Making her all but tremble with need. She felt as though her skin was overheated. Tingly and antsy. As if she was on fire. Her nipples prickled, demanding to be touched and she arched against him, pressing her breasts to his chest, desperate for some kind of contact. And still it wasn't enough.

Wrapping her arms around him, she twined her fingers into his hair and pulled him back just enough to ask, "Then why did you stay away?"

He gazed down at her, his eyes foggy with lust. "I don't know."

And for the life of her, she didn't know either. Honest to God, she couldn't think of one damn reason why they shouldn't be together. It had nothing to do with Peyton or the marriage. Nothing to do with her family or the rebellious tendencies she'd thought were long dead. This was about them. It had always been about them. And now that she was kissing him—now that his hands were all over her, making her tremble—she couldn't think of any reason why they should stay apart. When it was so obvious that they were meant to be together.

His lips moved from her mouth down to her neck, leaving a delicate trail of red-hot nibbles. She arched into his lips, all but praying he'd move lower and take her breast into his mouth.

"Oh, Jonathon," she murmured. "Please..."

She wasn't sure what exactly she was pleading for. Not when there were so many things she wanted him to do to her. So many places on her body she wanted him to touch and explore. All she knew was she wanted more. All of him.

Then abruptly, he let go of her and stepped away. Her body sagged with mounting desire, her legs limp and barely able to hold her up.

Thank goodness, she didn't need to support her own weight for long. His hand grasped her bottom, lifted her firmly against him and she automatically wrapped her legs around his waist. The position was perfect. Exquisite. As if her body had been precisely designed to wrap around his.

Her leggings were thin enough that she could feel the denim of his jeans through the delicate fabric. She felt every seam, every ridge. The hard line of his erection beneath his zipper pressed against the very center of her. She rocked her hips, increasing the pressure against her core, sending fissures of pleasure rocketing through her body.

He groaned low in his throat, still kissing her.

Then he pulled his mouth away from hers. "You're killing me here."

She grinned, brimming with pure feminine pride. "Am I?" she asked, shifting her hips again, delighting in tormenting him. But the sensation was too divine and she shuddered as well.

He muttered a curse that was half exasperation, half pride. "I shouldn't do this," he muttered. "I should be stronger than this, but I can't..." He nipped at her neck in a primal, animalistic sort of way that sent a shower of pleasure radiating across her skin. "I can't stay away any longer."

A second later, she felt him bump against the edge of his desk. He lowered her slowly down the length of his body. She didn't have even a moment to miss his warmth or the pressure against her sensitive skin, because he reached under the hem of her shirt and hooked his thumbs under the waistband of her tights and pulled them down her legs in one smooth movement, stripping away her panties as he did so.

She kicked off her shoes as she stepped out of her leggings, naked from the waist down. Her shirt hit her mid-thigh, but the fabric was gossamer thin and left her feeling scandalously exposed. Standing in her boss's office, half-naked, trembling with desire.

He stepped back to look at her. The heat in his

gaze made her skin prickle. Suddenly she was very aware of her hardened nipples pressing against the thin cotton of her bra. Of the moisture between her legs and the cool air on her thighs.

A feeling of vulnerability started to creep in under the heat of desire. Then she looked up and saw the expression on Jonathon's face. It was part dumb-struck awe and part reverent glee. Like a little boy standing in front of a Christmas tree, staring at the presents, wondering which one was his.

She brought her hands to the buttons running down the front of her shirt. Then flicked them free, one by one. His gaze stayed glued to the progression of her hands. He didn't move an inch. Except for his hands, which slowly curled into fists. As if it was all he could do not to reach for her and rip the shirt off her body himself. As if she was his deepest fantasy come to life.

For all she knew, maybe she was.

She wanted to think so. Needed to believe it. Because he was certainly hers.

It wasn't a fantasy she'd consciously entertained. Never something she dwelled on. Nevertheless, the idea of being with Jonathon, of seeing exactly this expression in his gaze…it had always been there. Right beneath the surface of her thoughts. Niggling at the edge of her awareness. She'd pushed it aside countless times. But now she pulled it from the depths of her mind and let it out into the light of day.

She wanted this. For years she'd wanted this. And now he was about to be hers.

Her hands reached the last button. She slipped it free of the buttonhole, letting the shirt fall open.

With a sweep of his arm, Jonathon knocked everything off his desk except for the blotter. Then he set her down carefully on the desk.

"You can't imagine the times I thought about doing this." He pressed a hot kiss to her neck as he nudged her shirt off one shoulder. "Every day." He nipped at her collarbone, sending hot spikes of desire radiating down through her chest. "I pictured you sitting here." His fingers popped open the front closure of her bra and peeled back the cups to reveal her bare breasts. "Right on my desk." Her bra dropped off and she arched her back as he trailed the tip of one finger from her collarbone down to her nipple. "Completely naked."

With a groan he dropped to his knees in front of her. As if he could no longer resist the temptation she presented. He parted her thighs, moved her bottom right to the edge of the desk and placed his mouth at the very core of her.

He devoured her in tantalizing licks. She dropped back onto her elbows, her eyes almost closed as wave after wave of pleasure washed over her. He was patient and thorough.

The pleasure was so intense that her eyes nearly rolled back in her head, but she couldn't make herself look away from the sight of his head between her legs, his close-cropped dark hair in such sharp contrast to her pale, quivering thighs.

Just when she thought she couldn't take it anymore, he focused his relentless attention on the tiny bundle of nerves so central to her pleasure, stroke after stroke, until she could hardly catch her breath. Then she felt his hand at her entrance. One finger, then two, plunged into her. She dropped onto her back, arching off the desk. As her climax crashed over her, she cried his name.

It felt like more than five years. Maybe his whole life he'd been waiting to see her like this. Spread out before him on the very desk that had so often been between them. She was the most delectable treat he'd ever sampled. Hot and moist with desire. Trembling from the aftereffects of a climax. His name still a whisper on her lips.

Now, here she was. Just like he'd always wanted. And he couldn't find a damn condom.

He had them here. Somewhere in the desk. Because he'd known for years how much he wanted her. And that some day he might act on it. Hell, there had been no "might" about it. With only the slightest hint of interest from her, he'd have acted on it. She needn't have stripped naked for him here in his office, though that certainly had been a dream come true.

And now he couldn't find the damn things.

He pulled one drawer out completely, dumping the contents on the floor. And then he did the same with the next drawer. And the next. Finally he found them, just when he thought the sight of her might make him come in his pants, just when his erection was twitching with the need to be inside of her.

When she saw what he'd been looking for, she was as eager as he was. He ripped open the package with trembling fingers, even as she unbuttoned his jeans and shoved them down around his hips. Then a second later, he was inside of her, her legs spread wide, her arms outstretched as she leveraged herself against the desk. Her hips bucked off the surface as he plowed into her over and over again. The feel of her body clenching around him was exquisite. The taste of her, still on his lips, was divine. But it was the sound of her cries of pleasure that sent his own climax rocketing through his body.

He knew in that moment, that he wanted her—just like this—forever. And that scared the hell out of him.

As soon as Wendy was able to move again, she sat up, pressing her face against his chest and wrapping her arms around him. She breathed in the musky scent of him. Relished the feeling of his taut muscles beneath her fingers and of his warm skin beneath her cheek. She wanted to sit like this forever, wrapped around him. Clinging to him. Her body still thrumming with pleasure. The feeling of complete and utter contentment cocooning her from the rest of the world.

But the world was out there and it wouldn't stay away forever. So when he stepped out of her embrace, she let him go, when what she really wanted to do was hold on fast.

She moved slowly, pulling her bra back on and then her shirt. Her fingers were still fumbling with the buttons when he spoke.

"This can't happen again."

Her head whipped up and she stared at him. He'd

turned away from her, but she could read the tension in his back as he zipped up his jeans. "Why not?"

"It's not a good idea." His voice was terse.

She felt that tension like a solid wall between them. She could feel him building it up. One brick at a time. One brick with each word. Part of her screamed that this wasn't the time for an argument. That the more they talked about it, the higher the wall would become, but she just couldn't let it go. It wasn't in her nature to back down from a fight.

"Not good for whom?" she asked.

"For anyone." He paused, then turned back to face her. His gaze drifted to her shirt, which hung open, her fingers having stilled midway up on their progress. "I'm afraid it'll be bad for you."

"Um, then you weren't paying attention," she said snarkily as she hopped off the desk. "Because that was extremely good for me."

She was naked from the waist down. True, her shirt was long enough that it hit her mid-thigh, but she still felt extremely exposed. Twenty minutes ago, before he'd rocked her world off its axis, that had been a good feeling. Now, not so much.

She swiped her tights off the ground, uncomfortably aware of how his gaze followed her every movement.

"Exactly. And good sex is addictive. You'll have a problem with that."

That cool, clinical tone of his made her blood pressure creep up. How the hell did he sound so calm? So rational?

"What kind of problem am I supposed to have with this…this extremely addictive sex?" And damn it, her tights were inside out. She rammed her hand down one of the legs, trying to snag the ankle hem so she could right them, but anger made her clumsy.

"I just don't think it's a good idea. It's not good for Peyton."

Watching Wendy's frustration grow as she wrestled with her tights, Jonathon wondered if perhaps he should have taken a different route.

"We're her parents now," she snapped, clearly exasperated. "I can't see how it would possibly hurt her for us to sleep together."

"You can't?" Why did she have to be so strong-headed? Why couldn't she just make it easier on both of them and agree with him for once?

"No. I can't. In fact, since we agreed that this marriage could last up to two years, I actually think it's a good idea."

"Then you haven't thought it through."

Of course, nothing was ever that easy. Not with Wendy.

One of the things that made her such a great assistant was that she never hesitated to give her opinion. No mindless agreeing for her. If she had a better idea, she said so. If she spotted a problem he'd overlooked, she pointed it out. Unfortunately, right now, it made her a pain in the ass.

Because what he really wanted—no, damn it, what he needed—was for her to stop talking about sex.

"Okay, maybe I didn't think it through." Finally—thank God—she got her tights right side out and stepped into them. "But now that I am, I don't know that I see a downside. Two years is a long time. And—" She broke off, appearing to grit her teeth before spitting out her next words. "And I'm not going to tell you that you can't see other people while we're married."

"Wendy—"

"No. Just let me say this, okay?" She swallowed visibly, not quite meeting his gaze, though he could tell she was mustering the gumption to do so. "I'm not going to forbid you from…doing what you need to do. But goodness knows, I'm not going to be registering on eHarmony anytime soon. So, maybe it's not a bad idea to—"

"What?" he asked. "To hook up anytime either one of us has an itch?"

She rolled her eyes. "What is wrong with you? Are you purposefully being the biggest jerk in history for a reason?"

"What is wrong with *me?* What's wrong with *you?*" He swept a hand toward his desk, as if displaying the destruction they'd done. "Five minutes ago we were having sex on that desk and now you're talking about me being with another woman? How is that normal?"

This had to be the most awkward conversation in his entire life. And considering that he sometimes talked to complete strangers about their finances, that was saying something.

She looked stricken by his words. Not for the first time either. She gave a little rapid blink, her eyes not quite reaching his gaze, and then swallowed. "I'm trying to be logical here. Two years is a long time and—"

"And you don't think I can keep my zipper up?"

Her gaze snapped to his face. "Let's just say, given that I've had a front-row seat to your dating practices for the past five years, I'm skeptical."

"Trust me. I can keep my zipper up."

She gave him a searing once-over. "All evidence to the contrary."

He gave her an icy, wolfish smile. "Is that really a stone you want to throw?"

"What do you want me to say? That I'm so impressed by your monkish fortitude?"

What *did* he want her to say?

He wanted her to say that she didn't want anyone else. That she wanted only him. And that she wanted him for some reason other than he was going to be convenient for the next two years.

"Okay, you want the truth? I don't think we should sleep together again, even if it means two years of celibacy. For both of us. I don't want you to get hurt, and you're too emotionally involved already."

"I'm too emotionally involved?" she scoffed, her voice dripping with sarcasm, but he could see the flash of pain in her gaze and knew he'd nailed it on the head. "*I* am? That's funny, because I wasn't the one just now who couldn't stop talking about how much I wanted this for the past five years. About how desperately I needed this."

Of course it would come back to that. He'd sounded like a lovesick fool. But neither of them would benefit from imagining he was some romanticized hero.

"Right," he said, bitterness seeping into his voice.

"I talked about how I wanted your body. How much I wanted you physically. Not how much I loved you." As he spoke, the tear that had been clinging to her lashes, finally gave up its battle and dropped down onto her velvety cheek. He gently brushed it off with his thumb, then held it up as evidence. "And I'm not the one crying now."

"You bastard. I can't believe you said that." She stepped back, putting some distance between them. "And you're wrong about one thing. I won't be begging to sleep with you again anytime soon. Not now."

She stormed off, but made it only as far as the office door before turning around. Propping her fists on her hips, she said, "I need to know now. Are you in or out?"

"What?"

"Are you in or are you out? Do you still want to do this, or are you wigging out on me?"

"I'm in," he said slowly. Undoubtedly deeper in than he should be.

"Are you sure? Because two years is a long time. And I'd rather know now if you're having second thoughts."

"I said I'm in."

"Good. My family wants to meet yours. They're

planning a reception for us. We leave for Palo Verde on Friday."

She didn't wait for his reply. It probably wouldn't have occurred to her that two years without sex wasn't nearly as off-putting as the idea of going to visit his family. A second later he heard the door to her office slam as she stormed out.

All alone in the office, he sank into his desk chair. Everything that had once been on his desk now lay scattered on the floor as well as the contents of three drawers. Years of keeping his life meticulously under control, of keeping his emotions neatly compartmentalized, and he'd blown it all in one reckless act.

He propped his elbows on his desk and dropped his head into his hands, ignoring the fact that his own cheeks felt suspiciously damp.

Thirteen

She wanted to stab him on her way out. There were several things in the office sharp enough to leave a nice puncture wound without being fatal. She took it as sign of great personal development that she didn't use any of them.

Then she sat in her car for several long minutes trying to hash out her feelings. Retrace her steps. Figure out where she'd gone wrong. In the end the only conclusion she could reach left her deeply unsatisfied.

Jonathon was right. She *was* too emotionally involved. She was up-to-her-tonsils-and-sinking-fast emotionally involved. Damn it.

Worse still, she couldn't follow her first instinct,

which was to run like a rabbit and hole up somewhere until she sorted through her emotions. No, with her family here, watching her like a hawk… Or maybe a pride of ravenous lions was a better analogy? Whatever hungry predator they were, she couldn't bolt. They'd attack at the first sign of weakness. She had to remember what was important. Keeping Peyton.

Then she thought of what she'd seen just yesterday morning. Jonathon sitting in the rocking chair with Peyton cradled in his arms. He may not know it yet, but she wasn't the only one who was emotionally involved.

He may not care about her—beyond her body, which he was obviously rather fond of—but he did care about Peyton.

Whether or not he wanted to admit it, he was a good father. He was a better father than he was a husband. Well, she could live with that. For the time being, she had to.

The days before the trip to Palo Verde passed quickly. Jonathon insisted she take the time off to visit with her family. Which seemed counterintuitive to her since the whole point of the marriage was to keep her at work. But every time she brought it up, he just stared at her stiffly and reminded her that taking off work to bond with Peyton would go a long way toward convincing them that she would be a good mother. He assured her that they still had plenty of time to work on the contract proposal. He, however, went stalwartly into work alone. He never again mentioned taking time off himself to play the part of the loving husband. Apparently—after they'd had sex at the office—that would have strained even his resolve. She assumed that when he said she should spend time with her family, what he really meant was that she should spend time with anyone other than him.

Truth be told, she let him put her off over and over, because she wanted to avoid the office too. She wasn't ready to be in the office where he'd made love to her with such abandon. Scratch that. Made love to *her body* with such abandon. And she damn sure wasn't ready to see him sitting behind the desk, working as if nothing had ever happened.

So she spent the days playing tour guide to her family. Mema was determined to hate everything about California and Big Hank flew back to Texas for the week, but her parents seemed to actually enjoy the time she spent with them. Even more shocking, she enjoyed it too.

She assumed that would change by the end of the week, when Big Hank, Hank Jr. and Helen would arrive. Helen had insisted on planning the wedding reception Mema had suggested the Morgans host. Without even leaving Texas, Helen had arranged a venue, invited guests and booked lodgings for the Morgans, which was no small feat to accomplish in just a few days' time. Whenever Wendy offered help, she was firmly rebuffed. Helen had even located and invited Jonathon's family. Though, apparently, only his older sister, Marie, had returned Helen's phone calls.

Wendy could hardly blame Jonathon's family. By the end of the week, she was sick of talking to Helen. The only thing worse than dealing with her was dealing with Jonathon.

At the end of each day, he'd arrive home and she'd have to—once again—pretend to be a loving wife. With the tension between them as strong as it was, she doubted she fooled anyone. Jonathon, however, did a bang-up job. She could barely turn around without having him there to touch her. To wrap his arm around her shoulder and drop a careless kiss on her forehead.

The nights were the worst. She could make it all the way through the day, she could even pretend in front of her parents, but her stomach knotted every time they closed and locked the bedroom door. She didn't know if her family found it odd for them to be locking the door, but she didn't dare risk having them walk in unannounced and seeing his pallet at the foot of the bed, where he'd been sleeping. The closest they came to communicating was the moment each night when she threw the pillow at him. Unfortunately, he always caught it. Damn him.

And before she knew it, it was Thursday. The week had slipped by and they'd be driving out to Palo Verde in the morning.

She lay there in the dark, unable to sleep and staring at the ceiling, irritated by the rhythm of his slow, even breathing from the foot of the bed. Thirty minutes passed. Then another twenty. Then she heard him roll over and sigh.

"Are you still awake?" she whispered in the dark.

"Of course. I'm on the floor and you're tossing and turning so much it sounds like a bounce house over there."

She bolted upright and snapped on the bedside lamp. "Would you just get into bed."

He blinked up at her, wedging his elbows under him. "Turn off the light. Try to get some sleep."

"I'd be able to sleep better if I didn't know you were uncomfortable sleeping on the floor."

He lay back down and stared up at the ceiling. "It's not that bad."

"It's two blankets and a pillow. It can't be good. You'll be safe sleeping in the bed. I'm not going to attack you or anything."

"It's just better if we limit our contact as much as possible. I'm trying to be noble here."

"Yeah." She snorted, falling back onto the bed. "I think that ship sailed the day we had sex on your desk."

"You're going to wake up Peyton."

Even though Big Hank had left, they'd decided to keep Peyton's crib in their room. She'd slept so much better when she was only a few inches away from them.

And though she knew Jonathon had a point—winning the argument wasn't worth waking Peyton, who would want to be fed in a few hours anyway—it only irritated her more. She yanked her pillow out from under her head and threw it at him. There was a satisfying whump as it landed on his torso.

"I already have a pillow."

"I know. I just wanted to throw something at you."

"Very mature."

"I know." Smiling, she snapped off the light.

He brought the pillow back to her, standing next to her side of the bed in the dark and holding it out to her. "I don't need it."

"Keep it. Maybe it'll make the floor a little less uncomfortable."

"Wendy—" he growled.

"I'm trying to be *noble.*"

"Fine," he snapped and went back to lie down.

It was wrong how pleased she was by the irritation in his voice. He may act as if he was completely indifferent to her, but she was still able to get under his skin. That shouldn't make her happy. But it did.

A few minutes later, she fell asleep smiling. And woke up in the morning with the pillow under her head.

At eighteen, Jonathon had left Palo Verde with $5,168.36 in his checking account—all earmarked for living expenses. His only other possessions were a partial scholarship to Stanford, two suitcases, a desk lamp, a used laptop, a backpack and a veritable mountain of student loans. He'd hitched a ride from their hometown to the coast in Matt's BMW. Jonathon hadn't been back since.

Palo Verde was a small but historic town on the

highway between Sacramento and Lake Tahoe. When he'd left in the mid-nineties, it was only just beginning to climb out of the economic slump that had cursed it since the gold rush ended more than a hundred years before. Now Sacramento had grown enough—and was expensive enough—for people to commute from Palo Verde. On a purely intellectual level, Jonathon supposed Palo Verde wasn't such a bad place to live. The town had a certain charm to it. Not the sort that any teenage boy would appreciate, but surely plenty of people liked musty old buildings and the gently rolling foothills of the Sierra Nevada mountains.

Nevertheless, during the drive Jonathon practically itched to turn the car around and get the hell out of there. If someone had asked him a month ago, he'd have sworn that nothing short of the coming apocalypse would have enticed him back to Palo Verde. Maybe not even that. If the world was coming to an end, why would he go there?

As they entered Palo Verde, with Peyton safely nestled in her car seat in the backseat, and Wendy beside him in the front, Jonathon clenched his hands so tightly around the steering wheel that he feared he might snap it in half. Sure, it was unlikely, but if anything was going to imbue him with Incredible Hulk-like powers, it would be this.

Wendy's family was in the rented minivan behind them on the highway. She sat with her iPhone, carefully dictating directions from the GPS map, as if he hadn't spent the first eighteen years of his life trapped in this God-forsaken hellhole.

"Okay," she said in a half whisper since Peyton was asleep. "It looks like this road will merge with Main Street just ahead."

"I know."

She ignored him. "And then, a couple of miles into town, Cutie Pies will be on your left."

"I know."

"It looks like there's parking on the street, but according to Claire's email, it fills up pretty quickly, so if we don't get a spot, we should circle around to the back of—"

"I. Know."

Wendy dropped the phone in her lap and held up her hands. "Hey, I'm just doing my part as navigator."

"I grew up here." He blew out a slow breath, prying the fingers of his left hand off the steering wheel and giving them a flex. "I don't need a navigator."

"Things can change a lot in fifteen years."

He didn't need her to tell him that. He was a completely different man than the boy who'd left town straight out of high school. He'd always thought it odd that spending his whole life wanting to escape from Palo Verde, he'd end up living in a city with such a similar name. Of course, Palo Alto was a completely different kind of town. The bustling intellectual hotbed of technological development. A city with many brilliant, very rich men. And he was one of them. So there was no reason at all that just breathing Palo Verde air should stir all his rebellious instincts. Yet it did.

It made him twitchy with energy and shortened his already strained temper. As if she sensed his mood—not that he was doing a great job of hiding it or anything—Wendy reached out a hand and gave his leg a stroke that she probably meant to be soothing. "It's just been a while since you've been back. I was trying to help."

He could feel the heat of her hand through the fabric of his jeans and it made his thigh muscles twitch. Instantly, he knew what he really wanted. The one thing that would expel all the anger and tension roiling inside of him. Sex. Good, clean, emotionless sex would do the trick. He could skip the drive through town to Cutie Pies and head up to the hairpin turns of Rock Creek Road, pull off into the trees, tug Wendy onto his lap and screw her right here in the front seat.

It was a good plan if he ignored the baby sleeping in the back of the car. It'd be even better if he didn't know emotionless sex was impossible with Wendy.

And then there was the minivan full of in-laws behind them. And the wedding reception Wendy's helpful cousins had planned for them.

He took little pleasure in knowing that once the wedding reception was over, he could leave Palo Verde and never look back. It didn't even help knowing that tomorrow Matt, Claire, Ford, Kitty and Ilsa would arrive for the reception. Having his best friends and their families there would make things better, but only a little bit. Before he could get through that reception tomorrow night, he still had lunch at Cuties Pies—that part wouldn't be bad. But he'd begun to wish he'd refused to come into town the day before the reception. Two whole days in his hometown was way too long.

It meant a lot of time dreading meeting with his family. Oh, he knew it was unavoidable. That was—after all—the sole purpose in having a wedding reception in Palo Verde. But he certainly didn't relish the idea.

In short. It sucked. The whole situation sucked.

He'd been acting like an ass ever since they'd had sex in his office. Of course, he didn't need Wendy's faux armchair psychology degree to figure out why. He was pushing her away every chance he got. Now if he could just get her to actually *go* away. So far, she wasn't budging.

He knew there were infinite explanations for the tenacity with which she clung to their relationship. The very fact that she was desperate enough to marry him in the first place was testament to that. With her family hovering nearby for the past week, she couldn't very well boot him out the door. And then there were those defiant urges of hers. She'd said it herself. For a woman from an old oil family, a man who made his money from green technology was the ultimate rebellion.

He'd been trying all week to distance himself emotionally from her, and he'd only made things more awkward. Since actively driving her away didn't seem to be working, it was time to own up to his mistakes. "I'm sorry. I just—"

"You're sorry?" She laughed. "Why on earth are you sorry? It's not your family who's bullied us into this stupid reception. I'm the one who should be apologizing."

"No, I've been acting like a jerk."

"No argument there," she muttered.

"And it's been worse for the past couple of days. I just—" Why was this so hard to say aloud? "I just don't look forward to having you meet them."

"Them?" she asked, her brow furrowing in confusion.

"My family."

"Why? Because my family's so great? With the manipulation and the backstabbing?"

"But they're…" he let the sentence trail off, realizing how it would sound.

"They're what?" When he didn't answer, she arched a brow. "They're rich. That's what you were going to say, isn't it? You think wealth excuses bad behavior? Well, it doesn't."

"That's not what I meant."

"Then what are you afraid of? Do you think I'm going to think less of you once I meet your family? Once I see firsthand that you grew up in poverty?"

There was enough indignation in her voice that he knew better than to say yes. That's exactly what he was afraid of.

As he pulled the car to a stop at a light, she shifted in the seat so she half faced him. "Be forewarned, I don't care about your past or where you came from, but the rest of my family might. And Helen is a real piece of work. If she thinks she can make you look bad by yanking the skeletons out of your closet, she'll do it. Just remember, no matter what she says, the fact that you come from a poor family doesn't make you less worthy in my eyes. It makes you more worthy. Yes, my family is wealthy, but so what? I didn't have to work for any of that money. You've worked for every penny you have. In my book, that says a lot."

Listening to her words loosened some of the anxiety in his chest. He could almost believe that she was right. And that where he came from made him a better man.

Almost. But not quite.

Fourteen

She'd heard a lot about Cutie Pies, but most of it had been from Matt. Considering that his wife owned the place, she'd expected all the praise to be exaggerated, but was pleased to find that it wasn't. It was a classic small-town diner on main street. It could have been found in any town in the United States. But rather than the standard greasy-spoon fare, the food was fresh, tasty and unique. However, at lunch, none of that made up for the tension hovering over the table like a dense, poisonous gas.

The atmosphere—compliments of Helen—was largely due to the fact that she'd invited Jonathon's sisters and brothers to the lunch without mentioning it to him or to her.

What had promised to be a stressful meal anyway was made even worse by Helen's interference. They arrived at the restaurant to find Helen and Hank Jr. out in front. Helen—as always a picture of moneyed, blond sophistication—looked horribly out of place in the homey diner. She gave air kisses to everyone, then linked arms with Mema and sashayed through the front door, the chime over her head tinkling, ringing the death knell of any hope Wendy had that this visit would go smoothly.

"I tried to call from the jet to reserve a table," Helen was saying, "but apparently, this little place doesn't even take reservations."

Wendy surveyed the restaurant with its simple red upholstered booths and gleaming bar stools. "It's a diner," she said dryly. "Of course it doesn't take reservations."

The interior of Cutie Pies was clean but worn, the staff friendly but unsophisticated. Wendy instantly loved it. Helen—who would turn up her nose at anything just to show she could—offered strained smiles, as though it was a horrible burden to be forced to eat in such a place. She didn't bother to hide it when she pulled an antiseptic wipe from her Gucci bag and gave the table a quick scrubbing before letting anyone sit down.

Then before anyone even had a chance to look over a menu, she hopped back up, standing behind Hank Jr. and talking as though she were hosting an elaborate dinner party.

"H.J. and I just want to thank y'all for coming for this reception we're throwing for our little Gwen."

Jonathon leaned close and whispered, "*Their* little Gwen?"

Wendy shot him a surprised look at the obvious amusement in his voice. Apparently poking fun at Helen's extravagant efforts to stay in the spotlight was enough to dissolve the tension between them.

Secretly pleased, she whispered back, "Fair warning—if you ever call me 'your little Gwen,' I'm stabbing you in the leg with a pickle fork."

Peyton sat in a high chair between them, happily gurgling away on a ring of rubber keys. Jonathon smiled and their eyes met over Peyton's head. For that moment—with Helen spewing utter nonsense at the end of the table, surrounded by her family with all their ridiculous eccentricities—she felt a bone-deep connection to Jonathon. Somehow, being with him made all of this—this weird family stuff she was having to deal with—seem more manageable. Yes, her family was overbearing, controlling, borderline obsessive. But for the first time, she felt strong enough to handle it. Because he was here with her.

That's when it hit her. She loved him.

This newfound feeling of being at peace with her family—hell, with the whole world—was due to him. Having him in her corner made her believe that she was capable of anything.

Wendy shook her head, rattled by the sudden—and damn scary—insight. At the head of the table, Helen said something that she must have intended to be funny, because she gave a tittering laugh. Peyton let out a loud squawk of protest. To calm her down, Wendy reached a hand over to pat her on the back. From the other side, Jonathon did the same and their hands touched. For an instant, they both stilled. Then Jonathon brushed his thumb across the back of her hand. Such a simple gesture, but the first time he'd voluntarily touched her since they'd had sex at the office.

A feeling of calm swept over her. They were going to be all right. Sure, they'd have some tough times ahead, but they could work through them. She was pretty sure. She tried to keep her smile to herself, but didn't quite manage it.

But then she glanced at Jonathon and realized he'd gone stone still. His gaze was pinned to a woman by the door. She was dressed simply in worn jeans and a T-shirt. Her hair was long and dark, with an inch-thick gray streak arcing over her forehead. She looked both earthy and beautiful. And her eyes were the exact same shade as Jonathon's.

"Oh, good!" Helen clapped her hands. "You must be Jonathon's sister, Mary. It's nice to meet after all the emails exchanged."

"Marie," the woman said, her gaze sweeping over the cluster of tables that now dominated Cutie Pies.

"I was afraid no one from Jonathon's family would make it." Helen made a grand show of bustling over to Marie. She hesitated, as if trying to figure out how to give Marie a welcoming hug without actually touching the other woman. She settled on giving an air kiss in the vicinity of Marie's cheek. "Welcome to the family."

Marie arched a brow, practically sneering her derision.

Wendy liked her instantly.

Unfortunately, it was obvious that Jonathon did not feel the same way.

Marie had never liked rich people. Of course, under these circumstances, Jonathon couldn't blame her. Helen was pretentious and obnoxious. She clearly thought she was better than Marie—probably better than everyone in the whole town—and she didn't bother to hide it.

Jonathon wasn't surprised that after all these years, Marie could still get her nose bent out of shape so easily. He also wasn't surprised that she was the only one in his family who would bother to show up. Family was everything to Marie. Even for family that had long ago deserted her.

Still it was obvious she didn't want to be there, in everything from the way she ordered nothing but tea, to the generous space she managed to wedge between her seat and the others near her.

Helen seemed doggedly determined to ignore the tension that hung over the table.

"So, Marie," Helen said brightly. "Tell us what you do."

Marie shot an annoyed look at Jonathon, as if he was somehow to blame for the inquisition. "I stay at home with my kids."

"Oh," was all Helen could say.

"What, you don't think that's real work?"

"No. I—" Helen fumbled for an answer. Jonathon couldn't help but enjoy her discomfort. After all, she had it coming. "I stay at home with my children myself. I know what a big job it is."

Beside him, Wendy snorted into her iced tea, trying to hide her laughter and keep from spewing her drink. Hadn't Wendy said Helen's kids went to boarding school?

Wendy stepped in to rescue Helen before she made an even bigger ass of herself. "Marie, will more of Jonathon's family be able to make it to the reception tomorrow? We'd love to meet his parents."

Marie shot him a confused frown. "Our dad died when Jonathon was in high school."

He felt, rather than saw, the stillness sweep over Wendy. "Oh. I'm sorry to hear that."

He should have told her. Of course he should have. But it wasn't the kind of thing that came up in normal conversation and he'd never particularly wanted to talk about it with anyone.

"Cancer," Marie said. "Probably from all those chemical pesticides."

"Oh," Helen said, trying to smooth over the awkward pause. "Is your family in agriculture?"

"Our dad worked in the apple orchards, if that's what you mean, but I wouldn't fancy it up by saying he was *in agriculture*."

"I see." Helen managed to sound almost sympathetic, but the faint glimmer of satisfaction in her eyes ruined the effect. "And your mother?"

"She lives in Tucson now, with her sister."

"And are there other siblings?" Helen asked.

Beside him, Wendy stared sightlessly down at her plate. He could practically read her mind. All the things he hadn't told her about his family were coming back to bite him on the ass. And there wasn't a damn thing he could do about it. He couldn't very well call a time-out, pull her back into the kitchen and pour out his whole miserable life's story. Even if he was the kind of the guy who would do that.

Before Marie could answer, Jonathon cut in. "Enough, Marie." Marie sharpened her gaze into a glare and looked as if she wanted to respond, but he didn't let her. "Enough acting defensive. If you're mad at me for not visiting more often or whatever, fine. We'll talk about it later." He turned his gaze on Helen next. "And enough from you too."

Helen looked as if she'd been slapped. He suspected that it was rare for anyone to put her in her place. "I never—"

"If you want to know about my family, ask me. Chances are, none of us are going to meet with your approval. My father worked in the orchards. My mother checked groceries. There are a lot of babies born out of wedlock. A sprinkling of jail time, but no felons. On the bright side, all of my nieces and nephews who are old enough have graduated from high school and most of them have gone to college. On scholarship. Not many families can say that. All in all, we're mostly just hardworking people you'd look down your nose at." He swept his gaze from Helen to the rest of the table. "Any other questions?"

No one spoke. After several seconds of silence, he pushed his chair back and said, "Wendy, why don't you grab Peyton and we'll go check into the hotel."

He dropped some cash by the register on the way out and waited for her on the sidewalk.

The second he left Cutie Pies, he knew it was a mistake. People like Helen were emotional vultures. Once she saw his vulnerabilities, she'd be circling overhead until something else brought him down. Then she'd pick over his carcass.

There was a bench out on the sidewalk, just a few steps away from the door to the diner, but still out of view of the interior. He sank to the bench and propped his head in his hands.

"That was brilliant, by the way."

He looked up to see Wendy standing there, Peyton on her hip, purse slung over her shoulder.

"That was stupid," he replied.

"No. Brilliant. Helen needs to have someone stand up to her occasionally. She puts on airs too often. If she knew how much Mema hated it, she wouldn't do it." Wendy gave a sly grin. "Which, I suppose is why I've never told her that Mema hates it."

"It was still stupid." He stood, rolling his shoulders to release some of the tension there.

"No, I agree with Wendy," came a voice near the door.

Jonathon looked around Wendy to see Marie standing just behind Wendy. "You know how I feel about putting people in their place."

"Yes, I do. I'm just not sure the patented Bagdon method of dealing with things is the way to go."

"What?" Marie asked. "The old beat-the-crap-out-of-someone-until-they-agree-with-you wouldn't work on her?"

He chuckled, despite himself.

"Look," Marie said, taking a step closer and giving him a little pat on the cheek. "It was good to see you. Even if it meant putting up with Ms. Snooty-pants in there."

Marie turned and headed down the block.

"Wait!" Wendy called out. "Won't we see you tomorrow at the reception?"

Marie sent her an amused look. "No offense, but no Bagdon is going to set foot in the country club. It's just not going to happen."

"But—"

"Sorry. It was nice to meet you."

Wendy watched Marie walk away for a second before thrusting Peyton into Jonathon's arms and rushing after her. "Then where should we have it?"

"Excuse me?" Marie stopped and looked at Wendy as if she'd grown another head.

"Forget Helen and her stupid ideas about a wedding reception. The only point in actually having a reception—and having it in Palo Verde—is so that I can meet Jonathon's family. If none of them will come to the country club, then I would like to know where we should have the party so that his family will come."

Marie looked warily at Jonathon, undoubtedly trying to figure out if Wendy was serious. All he could do was shrug. After all, he couldn't very well tell either woman that the last thing he wanted was to see his family again, let alone introduce them to his new wife.

"Isn't the party tomorrow night?" Marie asked. "You won't be able to plan a new party in twenty-four hours."

Wendy just grinned. She nodded toward him. "I keep FMJ organized and running. This will be a breeze."

Marie looked from Wendy to him and then back again, but she still looked doubtful. "Okay. If you want…" Marie got a shifty look in her eyes, one he remembered all too well from his childhood. She'd always had a knack for pushing boundaries and his gut told him that just now she was going to see how far she could push Wendy. "You should have it at my house."

"Marie—" he warned.

"I can't ask you to do that," Wendy said, cutting him off. "It's too much of an imposition."

"Or…" Marie said archly, "you think my house won't be nice enough."

He watched Wendy carefully, curious whether she'd pick up on Marie's subtle manipulation.

"No, no!" Wendy began. "That's not what I meant."

But Marie ruined whatever advantage she might have had by letting just a hint of smug satisfaction creep into her smile.

Wendy caught it. For the briefest second, she looked puzzled, but she recovered quickly. "I'm sure your house is lovely. What time would you like us to be there?" She didn't give Marie a chance to answer, but linked arms with the other woman and began walking toward the back parking lot, where Marie had been headed before Wendy had stopped her.

Jonathon had little choice but, with Peyton in his arms, to fall into step behind the two women and observe the battle of wills from what he hoped was a safe distance.

"Do you want me to try to find a caterer?" Wendy asked.

"A caterer?" Marie said the word as if it was a curse.

Jonathon would bet she'd never had a catered meal in her life.

"No, you're right," Wendy responded. "If Jonathon's family would be offended by the ostentation of the country club, then a caterer wouldn't be good either. We'll just show up with food, if you don't mind us using your kitchen. My mother is an excellent cook. And my father and Big Hank make some of the best barbecue in the state. Texas, that is." She flashed a bright smile. "Of course, we'll have to arrive early for that. Say, seven?"

"In the morning?" Marie squeaked. "You might as well stay with us overnight."

Wendy pretended not to hear the sarcasm in Marie's voice. "Jonathon and I would love that! We'll come over as soon as we get the rest of my family settled at the hotel. I assume Jonathon knows where the house is?"

Marie looked as though she'd been sideswiped by a fast-moving vehicle. "It's the house he grew up in."

Marie stopped in front of an old Ford. The car was worn, with a dented bumper and enough scratches that it looked as if it had been mauled by a lion. There were booster seats in the back and toys littering the floorboard.

"Great! We'll get my family settled at the hotel and see you in a few hours." Wendy launched herself at Marie and gave her a hug. "I've always wanted a sister."

Wendy stood beside him, her arm around his waist and her head resting on his shoulder while they watched the flabbergasted Marie back out of the parking lot and drive away.

As soon as the car was out of sight, Wendy straightened and sent him an exasperated look as she took Peyton back from him. "You should have warned me how things were between you and your siblings."

He shrugged. "You were the one who's been so sure you know me."

She considered his words and then nodded. "Okay. Fair enough." She studied him, her head cocked to the side, her expression pensive. "Do you ever see them at all?"

Instead of answering, he asked a question of his own. "You realize, don't you, that Marie didn't really invite us to stay with her?"

Wendy scoffed. "Of course I do. I'm not an idiot. But I'm not going to let her believe that we think she's not good enough."

"The last time I saw it, the house I grew up in was a total dump. It *isn't* good enough. Certainly not for your family."

"Let me worry about what's good enough for my family. Helen may be a fool, but…" She exhaled a long, slow breath. "Well, they're certainly difficult, but they know when to keep their mouths shut. And don't forget, Big Hank has been in politics for twenty years now. You don't get as far as he has without appreciating the hardworking middle class."

"But—"

Wendy cut him off. "Come on, we don't have time to debate it. We've got an impromptu wedding reception to plan."

She turned and headed back to the restaurant, but he snagged her arm as she passed. "What exactly is it you think you're doing here?"

She arched an eyebrow. "Isn't it obvious?"

"Unfortunately, it is. You think you're going to repair my relationship with my family."

She shrugged. "Well, somebody has to."

"No." He dropped her arm and shoved his hands deep into his pockets. "No one has to do it at all. My relationship with my sisters and brothers is nobody's business but mine. Stay out of it."

"I'm not going to." She said stated it so simply, only a hint of condescension in her voice. "This is your family. I'm not going to stay out. You obviously regret how strained your relationship with them is. Someone has to bridge the gap."

"And what exactly is it you think you're going to gain by doing this for me? You want me to be thankful? You want me to drop down onto my knees in gratitude? What do you expect?"

A tiny frown creased her brow, as if she didn't understand the question. "I expect you to be happy."

"Mending the rift between me and my family isn't going to make me happy."

"Are you sure?" She cupped his jaw with her hand, her blue-violet eyes gazing up into his with such compassion it nearly took his breath away. "Because you want to know what I think? I think you've never forgiven yourself for walking away from them. I think, when you left to form FMJ, you never looked back and that you've always regretted it."

"If I did walk away from them and never looked

back, maybe it's because I don't want them in my life. Did that ever occur to you? Maybe I'm just a selfish enough bastard that I want to enjoy my wealth and success without any reminders around of where I came from."

"I don't believe that."

"You don't have to believe it for it to be true."

"You know what I *do* believe? I believe you don't have any idea how to bridge the gap between you, so you just let it stand."

He didn't know what to say, didn't know how to convince her that she was spinning fantasies about him that just weren't true. And whatever words he might have used to convince her got choked in his throat anyway. So he said nothing and let her continue talking.

"I've seen you with Peyton. I know how good you are with her. How caring. And I know you must have felt that same way about your family. Your real family. I think you haven't married and had kids of your own because it's your way of punishing yourself for abandoning them. That's the real reason you wanted to marry me. By marrying me, you could lie to yourself about your motives, but you'd still have the family you've always wanted."

"That's bull." He said it with more conviction than

he felt. "I married you because FMJ fell apart without you. But don't think that the freedom you have in running FMJ's office extends to meddling in my personal life."

"What personal life?" she scoffed. "That's the point, isn't it? That's why none of your romantic relationships last longer than a financial quarter and why Matt and Ford are your only friends."

He wasn't even going to dignify that with a response. Instead, he stalked toward her until she backed up a step and then another. "I'm going to make this real simple for you. Back off."

"No."

"No?" He stopped, flabbergasted by her gall. "What do you mean, no?"

"I mean, no, I'm not going to back off."

"Why the hell do you even care about this?"

"Because we're married now. And I care about you." She crossed her arms over her chest, bumping up her chin as if she was challenging him to argue with her. "There. I said it. I care about you and I want you to be happy. I don't think this—this thing where you cut yourself off from everyone is going to make you happy. So I'm going to do everything in my power to fix it." She took a step closer to him and gave his chest a firm poke. "And unless you want to fire me, admit to everyone that our marriage was a ruse and give me an annulment right now, there's not a damn thing you can do about it."

With that, she turned on her heel and marched away, back around the corner to Main Street and back to her family waiting for them in Cutie Pies. Where presumably she'd announce her plan to move the wedding reception to Marie's house. All in the interest of repairing familial bonds.

Ah, crap.

This marriage thing was ending up to be much more work than he'd anticipated.

Fifteen

Jonathon did not want to spend the afternoon becoming reacquainted with his big, sprawling mess of a family.

He did not want to spend the night in the tiny, three-bedroom, two-bathroom tract house where he'd grown up.

Hell, he didn't even want to leave the comfort of Palo Verde's one luxury hotel. Luxury being a somewhat fluid term. In this case, meaning historic, not decrepit and possessing a well-stocked bar.

After lunch, he'd drawn out the afternoon as much as possible, his annoyance with Helen surpassed only by his aversion to spending more time with his own family. So he showed Wendy's family around town, lingering over checking them into the hotel. Anything to avoid bringing Wendy to his sister's house.

Which was why he was now hiding out in the bar, waiting for Wendy to walk her grandmother back to her room.

He sat there, the ice-cold Anchor Steam almost untouched in front of him, considering his options for getting out of sleeping on his sister's living-room floor on a blow-up bed.

While the place may or may not be quite the dump it had been when he was growing up, it was still smaller than his sister's five kids needed. And for some reason he'd never understood, his sister doggedly clung to the damn thing. While he didn't keep in touch with any of his siblings, he kept tabs on them and their finances. He didn't want to be involved in their lives, but he didn't want any of them out on the street either. And he'd made sure his sister could afford better if she wanted it. Apparently she didn't.

Now he wished he'd given up on being subtle and respecting her pride and had just bought her a damn mansion. Hell, maybe it wasn't too late. What were the chances he could find a twenty-four-hour Realtor?

He took one last swig of beer and then pushed away from the mostly full bottle. Before he could even stand up, Big Hank sauntered in.

"Thank God, you're here." Big Hank pulled back a chair for himself without waiting for an invitation.

"Is something wrong?" Jonathon asked, poising to head for the door if there was.

"No, no," Hank muttered. The big man pulled off his cowboy hat and settled it onto one of his knees. "I just hate to drink alone." Then he laughed as if he'd told the funniest joke.

Jonathon smiled, humoring the older man until the waitress could come over to take his drink order. For the first few minutes, while they were waiting, Hank spun his particular brand of good-ol'-boy charm.

Jonathon was too wise to underestimate him. Instead he said little and mostly listened to one over-the-top story after another. He knew better than to take the stories seriously. But also knew that every word out his mouth could be the truth. With a guy like Big Hank, just about anything was possible.

Just as Jonathon was finishing his beer and about to make his excuses, Hank settled back, stretched an arm along the back of his side of the booth and said, "But enough about me." If the past thirty minutes were any indication, he wasn't a man who could ever say enough about himself. "I want to talk to you about Gwen."

Something in his tone gave Jonathon pause. "What about her?"

Hank gave the ice in his scotch glass a little swirl. "When you left the restaurant today, Mema sent me to find you. I overheard your conversation in the parking lot."

Which could mean almost anything, depending on how much of the conversation Hank had heard. "And?"

"And I know your marriage is a sham."

"And?" Jonathon asked again.

"You know what I think? I think Gwen put you up to this. I think she's trying to worm her way into Mema's good graces, so she can avoid a custody battle." Hank chuckled, raising his glass as if in toast to Wendy's ingenuity. "What I couldn't figure out at first was how she roped you into going along with her." Hank gestured with the glass he held in his hand. "You're a smart man. I doubt you'd get involved with this scheme of hers unless it benefited you."

"I love Wendy," Jonathon said, the rehearsed words sounding flat on his tongue.

"No," Hank muttered. "I don't think you do."

Jonathon leaned forward, propping his elbows on the table. "You can't prove I don't love her."

Hank took a gulp of his drink and gave his head a sharp shake of his head. "I think she convinced you that a marriage to her would benefit FMJ. I think that's how she got you to marry her."

"She didn't *get* me to marry her. I proposed."

Hank studied him for a moment, then his lips twisted in a sly smile. "FMJ does some extraordinary work."

The sudden change of topic gave Jonathon only a moment's pause. "What's your point?"

"I know you're putting together a big proposal for the Department of Energy. Those smart-grid meters of yours are mighty interesting. Matt said if y'all win this government contract, every government building in the country will be retrofitted with one of those meters. Could save the nation millions in electric bills."

"Matt wasn't supposed to show you the smart-grid meters."

"He got a little overenthusiastic. And I found them mighty interesting."

"And let me guess, if I do something you want, you'll make sure FMJ gets that contract?"

"No. Certainly not. That would be nepotism." He

scoffed as though the idea were repugnant. Then added, "But what I could do is make sure that the FMJ doesn't get the contract."

"And what do I need to do in return?"

"Get an annulment. Send Wendy home with her family."

"No," Jonathon said without even considering an answer.

"Just think about all those smart-grid meters of yours," Hank said, his voice taking on a slick and oily quality. "All those fantastic widgets of yours. Sitting in a warehouse, doing nothing."

"You're threatening me."

Hank smiled. "More to the point, I'm threatening FMJ. Make no mistake about it. If you walk away from this marriage, I can make fabulous things happen for you and for FMJ."

"But only if I walk away. From Wendy and from Peyton."

"Exactly."

"Just tell me this. Why? Why go to all the trouble to blacklist me over one tiny baby. Wendy thinks it's all about the money. But I don't believe that. Did Mema put you up to this?"

"No. All she really wants is for Wendy to visit

more often. She'd be happy with a promise to bring Peyton to Texas every once in a while."

"So why not just let Wendy raise her?"

Big Hank pinned him with a steely stare. "Now don't get me wrong, boy. I have a lot of respect for your Gwen. It takes some *cojones* to stand up for yourself in this family. And your Gwen certainly has a pair. Probably bigger than Hank Jr.—though Helen could give her a run for her money. The thing about Helen, at least I know how to control her. She always follows the money. But Gwen…Gwen's a loose cannon. She doesn't give a damn about the money."

Jonathon thought about Wendy and knew that her uncle was right, about the money at least. She didn't care about it. She cared about the baby. After a minute, Jonathon looked up to find Big Hank studying him. "What about me?" he asked.

Hank studied him shrewdly. "You're a businessman first and foremost. You haven't spent the last thirteen years of your life building a company from the ground up just to throw it away over a baby. Or even over a woman. You'll do what's right by FMJ."

Jonathon pretended to think about it. Mostly because Big Hank would never take seriously someone who would turn down his deal without considering it. Then he shook his head, chuckling a little under his breath. "You know, she said you'd do this."

Big Hank smirked. "Do what?"

"She said that her family always found a way to twist what someone wants. Turn it against them. Or rather turn them against her."

For a second, Big Hank looked as though he might deny the accusation. Then he just shrugged his shoulders and owned up to it. "Most of the time, she's made it easy. Wendy always dated men who were weaker than she was." Big Hank gave Jonathon a slow and assessing look. "But not you, son."

"No. Not me." He scraped a line of condensation off his beer bottle. "So tell me something. From what I understand, you tried to control your daughter, Bitsy, and in the end you only drove her away. So why are you trying to do the same thing to Peyton?"

"Why did the scorpion sting the turtle? It's in my nature. And people don't really change, no matter how they wish they could."

Jonathon pushed back his chair. "Well, sir, with all due respect, I've lived my whole life in Northern California. And I don't understand homespun analogies about scorpions. Never seen a scorpion in my life."

"Is that your way of telling me you're not going to take me up on my offer?"

"I suppose it is."

Big Hank arched a skeptical brow. "You fancy yourself in love with Gwen? You think you're going to impress her by turning me down?"

For one overly long instant, time seemed to stop. As if everything in his body came to a complete and utter standstill, but the rest of the world kept turning and slammed against him with full force.

Love? Was he in love with Wendy?

The idea was preposterous. Ludicrous.

And yet…

He shook his head, partly in answer to Big Hank's question and partly to dispel the very idea before it could take root in his mind. "No. I don't think this will impress her. I don't plan on her ever finding out about your offer."

"You know my offer goes both ways. I could guarantee you get the contract. I could make sure every government building in the country uses one of your smart-grid meters. Hell, I could get one in every house built in the next decade. Or I can guarantee that FMJ never sees another drop of government money. Not on this project. Not on any project. Ever."

"You make it sound so tempting. Would you like a swivel chair to sit in and fluffy white cat to stroke while you repeat it?"

For a second, shock registered on Big Hank's pudgy features. Then he burst out laughing. "You know, Jonathon, I like you. It's a shame you're not going to be my nephew-in-law."

"I'm not going to accept your offer."

"Not yet. But you will eventually. You'll sit down and think about it. Do the math—which won't take you very long, if what Gwen says about you is true. Once you realize how much money I'm talking about, you'll come around. No woman is worth that much money."

The truth was, he'd already been doing the math. Calculations had started running through his mind the second Big Hank had spoken. "Maybe you're right. Maybe no woman is worth that. But where you're wrong is in thinking that Wendy is the reason I'm saying no." Big Hank's gaze narrowed, but he didn't interrupt. "This thing you do, this good-ol'-boy manipulation, this under-the-table way of doing business—" Jonathon gave his head a shake. "It isn't FMJ's style. We do things out in the open. We win contracts because our products are the best on the market, not because we have connections. FMJ's an honorable company. We don't make the kind of deals you're talking about."

Big Hank leveled a shrewd look at him. "That may be FMJ's policy. But I've done my research on you. The kind of background you have makes a man hungry for success. If there's one thing my twenty-five years in politics has taught me, it's that there's not much an ambitious man won't do if you offer him the right incentives."

"I suspect you're right. About me. But I'm only one-third of FMJ. And you're wasting your time."

And with that, Jonathon turned and left.

He only wished he knew what drove him away: the fear that Big Hank was right and he really had made that decision for Wendy's sake, or the fear that if Big Hank kept talking, eventually Jonathon would cave. Either way, he figured he was pretty much screwed.

Sixteen

Knowing what she knew about Jonathon's childhood, Wendy half expected the house Jonathon grew up in to be a decrepit shack. But Marie's house was just an average tract house, in a neighborhood that may have been on the low end of middle class. Though small, the house was obviously well cared for, with a neat, flower-edged lawn in front. Bicycles and toys littered the yard, a testament to the number of kids who lived there.

Jonathon parked his Lexus out in front. He studied the house, his expression grim, his hands tight on the steering wheel.

To lighten the mood, she said, "Oh, you're right.

This place is horrible. A real dump. Maybe we should go get our hepatitis C shots before going in."

He glared at her. "It was worse when I was a kid."

"Everything always is." She could all too easily imagine how hard an impoverished childhood would have been on Jonathon, with his stubborn pride and his desperate need to control everything. She gave his thigh a pat. "Come on, let's go in."

She hopped out of the car, knowing he'd follow along if she forged ahead. By the time she'd removed the bucket car seat from the back, he was there to take it from her, but the tight line of his lips hadn't softened at all.

"Think about it like this…whatever happens, they can't be any worse than my family is." She meant to make a joke of it, but the oddest expression crossed his face. She frowned. "What?"

"Nothing." He shook his head, gripped the car seat a little tighter and headed across the street. "Let's get this over with."

"Great attitude, by the way," she muttered under her breath. But he ignored her, trudging up toward the house with such determination that she had to jog a few steps to catch up with him.

A moment later, the door was being opened by a

lovely young woman. Wendy guessed she was in her early twenties. She had Marie's dark glossy hair and the Bagdon green eyes. There was only a moment's hesitancy in her expression before she threw her arms around Jonathon. "Uncle Jonny! It's so good to see you!"

Shock registered on Jonathon's face, then slowly, he wrapped his free arm around her back. "Hey, Lacey."

Lacey pulled herself out of his arms and gave him a once-over. Nodding in apparent approval, she said, "You haven't changed a bit." Jonathon looked as if he wanted to disagree, but she didn't give him a chance. Instead she moved on to Wendy, giving her a hug that was just as enthusiastic. "You must be Wendy. Welcome to the family."

Then she darted off into the house, calling out, "They're here! Momma, why didn't you tell us she was so cute?"

Jonathon—looking shell-shocked—just stood there for a moment. So Wendy pushed past him to enter the house. "You coming, Jonny?"

His gaze narrowed. "Shut up," he muttered, but his tone was playful, which she figured was the best she could hope for under the circumstances.

Wendy met so many people in the next hour, she

quickly lost track of them. There was Lacey, the oldest of Marie's three kids. Or was it four? Then there were two additional step-kids as well. Neither of Jonathon's brothers had come—though Marie insisted she was still working on them and hoped they would be there for the big reception the next afternoon. His other sister came by and brought three of her four kids. Even Lacey's boyfriend was there.

Everyone greeted her warmly and oohed and aahed over Peyton. But Jonathon spent most of the evening standing stiffly in the corner, giving monosyllabic responses any time someone talked to him and looking deeply uncomfortable.

Photo albums were brought out and pizza was ordered. Someone brought soda and beer. Someone else brought cupcakes. Wendy could see why none of them would have wanted to go to a party at the country club and she was glad Marie had spoken up and told them so.

She was talking to Marie's husband, Mark, when Lacey came up and coaxed Peyton out of her arms. "I have to cuddle with babies whenever I can," she explained. "Mom's forbidden me to get pregnant until I'm at least three years out of college."

"Useful rule."

Lacey, however, was already ignoring Wendy in favor of rubbing her nose against Peyton's.

Wendy glanced around the busy living room and noticed that Jonathon was nowhere to be seen. She asked around and finally, one of the many children huddled around the video games being played on the TV yelled over his shoulder that Jonathon had gone out into the backyard.

She grabbed a sweater that was draped over one of the kitchen chairs by the back door on her way out into the darkened backyard. Slipping her arms into the sweater, she shivered as she waited for her eyes to adjust. The night air was cool against her skin. The unfamiliar landscaping cast deep shadows over the lawn. She skirted the furniture scattered around the tiny patio and stepped out onto the grass. In the light from the half-moon overhead she could barely see Jonathon.

Picking her away across the lawn around horseshoe sets and toy dump trucks, she crossed to where he stood beside a sapling tree.

He turned as she approached, studying her in the moonlight.

"Are they really so bad you had to come out here to escape?" she teased.

"I wanted to see if it was still here." He nodded

toward the tree. "I planted an acorn here on the day we buried my dad. I picked it up from the lawn at the cemetery."

Though the tree was taller than he was, it still looked gangly and young. "That tree couldn't be more than ten years old."

"Almost twenty years now," he said softly. "Trees grow more slowly than people do."

She nodded, but looking at him, wondered if that was true. Sometimes, it felt as if people didn't grow at all. "I don't know about that," she admitted. "Here I am at twenty-seven, making the same mistakes I made at seventeen." She let out a dry bark of laughter. "And at seven."

"You sure about that?" he asked. "You seem to be getting along with your family pretty well these days."

"Maybe." She shrugged. "My mom said something the other day that surprised me. She said the reason Mema is so against single mothers is—"

"Because she was a single mother herself," Jonathon finished the sentence for her.

She shot him a surprised look. "How did you…?"

"Your Uncle Hank's father died in Korea. He was just six months old. She didn't marry your grandfather for another two years."

"And you know this…how, exactly?"

He raised his hand. "Fan of Google. Remember?"

"You researched my uncle?"

"Well, your family. There's a Wikipedia article on the Morgans. You're sort of a footnote."

"We live in a weird world." She just shook her head, wrapping her arms more tightly around her body. "I never thought to Google myself. If I had, I guess I would have known that about Mema and Uncle Hank's father."

"You didn't know?"

"It was only vaguely familiar. I must have heard it years ago and forgotten. I've never even heard Mema mention her first husband. And when Papa was alive he treated Uncle Hank and Dad like they were both his children. He set up trusts for all of us grandkids. Just like Hank Jr. and Bitsy were his own." She felt tears prickling her eyes, and blinked them back.

It had been so long since she'd thought about her Papa. He filtered through her thoughts nearly every day, but she didn't often take out the memories and dust them off.

"He used to love having the whole family together," she said, suddenly wanting to share those memories with Jonathon. "He loved the holidays most. When all the grandkids were running around. He'd have adored Peyton."

For the first time, it occurred to her that maybe the tenets of her trust hadn't been designed to control and manipulate her. Maybe he'd just wanted all the family to stay together forever. How disappointed he'd be.

Of course, he'd never met Helen. He probably wouldn't want to be around her either.

Still, the thought of Papa's disappointment snatched her breath away and she found herself shivering again.

Jonathon must have noticed. He unzipped his windbreaker and pulled her close so her back brushed against his chest. Then he wrapped the edges of the jacket around her, enveloping her in his warmth.

She leaned her head back against his shoulder, looking at the tree he'd planted so long ago, marveling that he'd planted a single acorn and it had actually grown into something. Not something big yet, but with the potential to someday be massive and strong.

"Tell me something, Wendy," he murmured, his voice close to her ear. "If there was a way for you to keep Peyton without being married to me, without moving back to Texas, would you do it?"

Everything inside of her went dead still at his question.

She squeezed her eyes shut again. This time, not to shut in tears but to block out her dread. She knew every modulation of his voice. The question wasn't pure speculation. She knew if she could see his face, he'd be wearing his I-solved-the-problem expression. Was he wondering—as she was—if this greater understanding of Mema could be used to convince her that Wendy was a suitable mother, with or without a husband?

"No," she admitted softly. Barely a whisper. She was not even sure she wanted him to hear it.

But he did hear it. She felt it in the faint stiffening of his muscles.

And a moment later, he stepped back from her and held out his hand. Nodding toward the house, he said, "It's almost Peyton's bedtime."

She let him lead her back across the lawn and into the boisterously cheerful company of his family. Although she smiled brightly as everyone said goodbye and started heading home, she couldn't dislodge the lump of dread in her throat.

She'd admitted to him that she'd stay married no

matter what, but he had—rather obviously—not done the same. And she couldn't help wondering, did he fully realize what she'd admitted? Did he know that she was already in love with him?

By the time Jonathon followed Wendy back into the house, Marie had noticed how sleepy Peyton looked and was beginning to shuttle people out the door. Wendy stood stiffly to the side, seeing people off. The bright smile on her face didn't quite reach her eyes. He wasn't sure what he'd done to upset her, but it was obvious that he'd made a mess of things.

Finally Marie showed Jonathon and Wendy to one of the bedrooms. There were bunk beds along one wall and—just as Jonathon had predicted—a blow-up bed on the floor. Marie had pulled a Pack 'n Play out of the attic and wedged it between the head of the bed and the room's only dresser. Toys had been piled up on the lower bunk bed to clear space on the floor for the blowup bed, which barely fit as it was. Unless one of them wanted to sleep on the top bunk, they'd be in the same bed tonight.

As soon as they were alone, Jonathon asked, "You sure you don't want to head back to the hotel?"

"I've stayed in worse," she said, her tone determinedly cheerful as she lay Peyton down on the bed and started to change her clothes.

He arched a brow. "Really?"

"Yes, really. I took a year off college to backpack around Europe." She dug through the suitcase and pulled out the pink footie pajamas Peyton liked. "I've even stayed worse places on FMJ's dime."

"I doubt that."

"Then you've obviously forgotten that hotel in Tokyo." With Peyton sitting on her lap, she began the complicated wiggle-and-giggle of dressing a squirming child. "The rooms were the size of shower stalls and the beds were too short even for me."

"I must have blocked it out."

"Yeah. I bet." She chuckled as she rolled Peyton onto her back to work on the snaps, leaning down to give the baby a raspberry on the belly. Peyton let out a sleepy squeal, kicking her arms and legs. Wendy zipped the pj's up and patted Peyton on the belly.

It was an action so intrinsically mothering it made his breath catch in his throat. He knew in that instant that she was going to be okay. She and Peyton may have gotten off to a rough start, but they were going to be just fine. With or without him. He knew something else as well. He should tell her the truth about her uncle. Tell her what Mema really wanted.

It was such a simple solution. And if he told her, she wouldn't need him anymore.

She looked up to find him studying them and she frowned. "What?"

He gave his head a little shake. "Nothing. You're just getting good at that."

"Yep, that's me. Nearly a month of mothering under my belt and I've mastered the art of zerbert delivery."

"No. I mean it. You're going to be a good mother."

Despite the compliment, her frown deepened. She sat cross-legged on the center of the bed, her expression pensive as she picked up Peyton and set her on her knee.

The air between them was thick with all the things that had gone unsaid, but before he could say anything, she hobbled up, setting Peyton on her hip.

"Peyton and I are good here." She snagged the bottle she'd prepared earlier and gave it waggle. "We're all set. Maybe you should go hang out with your family for a while. While I get her to sleep, I mean."

"No. I—"

"I insist." She gave his shoulder a gentle shove.

Then for effect, she rubbed her finger along her brow as if she was warding off a headache. "This weekend has been really hard on me. I just want a few minutes alone with Peyton."

He saw right through the ruse, but he didn't call her on it. Maybe she needed time alone. Maybe she just needed time away from him.

He left the room, all too aware that he hadn't told her about her uncle. Nor had he mentioned that she probably didn't need to stay married to him in order to keep Peyton. He hadn't told her yet. And he wasn't going to.

Seventeen

Wendy had no more answers when she woke up than when she'd fallen asleep. And to make matters worse—after more than a week of waking at the crack of dawn and hightailing it out of the room, this was the morning Jonathon decided to sleep in. So she woke to find herself draped across his body, her head resting on his chest, her left knee nestled against the hard length of his erection.

There was a moment when she didn't quite remember where she was. When all her sleep brain could process was the unbelievable feeling of total contentment.

That moment passed in a flash the instant she felt him move. She shot off the bed.

Or rather rolled to the edge, only to feel the bed give way beneath her weight. She sank to the floor and tried to stand, but the bunk beds were in the way. She clung to the upper bed's railing, the lower bed bumping her legs as she inched her way to a spot of open floor space.

"Morning," Jonathon muttered.

She stilled, then looked over her shoulder. He was awake, watching her awkward progress. "Um, hey." His gaze dropped to her bottom. Suddenly aware of the cool air on the cheeks of her buttocks, she gave the hem of her boxers a tug. "Good morning."

He just smiled, looking awfully smug. The jerk.

She finally reached the foot of the bed where there was about a four-inch gap between it and the wall. She shuffled around until she reached the dresser.

"I'm just going to—"

She didn't even finish the sentence. She just grabbed her clothes and ran for it.

Ten minutes later, out of her skimpy pajamas, clothed in as many layers as she could scrounge and determined to buy a pair of long johns to sleep in from now on, she made her way to the kitchen and the divine scent of freshly brewing coffee.

She found Lacey there, a cup of steaming coffee at her own elbow as she greased up a waffle iron.

The younger woman smiled brightly. "Hope you're ready for the patented Bagdon Banana Chocolate Chip Waffles. You're a fan, right?"

Some wise person had left an empty coffee cup beside the coffee maker and Wendy poured herself a cup. "Of waffles? Sure."

"Not just waffles. These are the Banana Chocolate Chip Waffles. His signature dish."

Feeling unable to follow the discussion without caffeine, Wendy took a generous gulp. Whatever criticisms Jonathon might have had about his family, they brewed damn good coffee. Which in her book, about put them on the level with the gods.

A moment later, her brain caught up with the conversation. "Whose signature dish?"

Lacey, who was in the process of pouring a ladleful of batter onto the hot iron, looked up. "Jonathon's." She sprinkled chocolate chips across the top. "He has made them for you, right?" Lacey closed the lid, then pegged Wendy with her gaze.

"Um…no."

"Oh." The waffle iron released a fizzle of steam. A frown creased Lacey's forehead. "He used to make them all the time for me. He taught me how."

Caught off guard by the girl's wistful tone, Wendy was torn. The girl looked as though a cherished childhood memory had just been stolen. But Wendy couldn't exactly tell Lacey the truth. And for all she knew, Jonathon actually made waffles for all of his real girlfriends. He'd just never made them for his fake wife.

"Maybe," Wendy supplied, "he doesn't make them now because they remind him too much of you."

She couldn't imagine the Jonathon she knew behaving in such a sentimental manner, but the girl might fall for it.

Sure enough, Lacey's lips curved into a smile and she nodded slowly. "Yeah. That sounds like him."

"It does?" Wendy tried to hide her surprise behind a sip of coffee. "I mean, it does. Definitely."

The waffle iron beeped and Lacey bent down as she lifted the lid. Wielding a spatula with surgical precision, she pried the waffle free and flipped it onto a plate. She put on the finishing touches with a flick of a butter knife and drizzle of syrup, then held the plate out to Wendy. "Ta da!"

Wendy took the plate. Lacey stood there, her gaze darting from the waffle to Wendy and back like an overeager puppy.

"Now?" Wendy asked. "Shouldn't I wait until everyone else is here?"

"Nope. First come, first served, and you eat them

while they're hot." As she poured the next waffle, Lacey flashed a wicked grin that reminded Wendy of Jonathon. "House rules."

Imagine that. House rules about waffle eating. Or, for that matter, house rules about anything food related that weren't restrictive and oppressive.

"Are you going to try it?" Lacey asked, her forehead starting to furrow again.

"Just taking a moment to enjoy house rules about food that aren't designed to inspire guilt or shame. I think I'm in heaven."

"And you haven't even eaten the waffle yet."

Since Lacey was still watching her expectantly, Wendy forked off a bite and popped it into her mouth. The sweet buttery banana contrasted nicely with the dark bittersweet chocolate. The waffle itself was light enough to melt on her tongue. Her eyes drifted closed in bliss.

Even though Wendy hadn't said anything, beside her, Lacey said, "I know. Right?"

"Divine," Wendy enthused before taking another bite. If Jonathon *did* make these for his real girlfriends, that went a long way toward explaining why they put up with his emotional distance for as long as they usually did. These waffles plus fantastic sex, and what girl would care if her boyfriend was a jerk?

Somehow depressed by the thought, Wendy took her waffle and wandered over to the table. She scooted the chair back with her foot and sat, stuffing another bite into her mouth with a fervor that had more to do with therapeutic stress release than with hunger.

A moment later, Lacey joined her, a waffle of her own on her plate, the waffle iron temporarily off since no one else was waiting for one.

They ate for a few minutes in silence.

Lacey gave a sigh of deep contentment. "Uncle Jonny used to make these for me when I was little. Mom worked at the Giddey-up Gas on weekend mornings."

"You must have been…what? Six or seven?"

"I was eight when he went off to college."

Went off to college and walked away from his family completely. As far as she knew, he hadn't seen a single family member since then. Okay, she could get walking away from the no-good mother who had been more interested in raising a bottle than raising a family. But walking away from his siblings? She'd wanted a brother or sister her whole life. So that was a grayer area. But walking away from an eight-year-old niece? A little girl he'd made waffles for every morning for years? Who did that?

Had it been hard? Had he ever looked back? Ever wondered about the family he'd left behind?

"And you haven't seen him since?" Wendy had to ask, even though in her heart she knew the answer to the question.

"Not really." Lacey shrugged, though her expression was more thoughtful than sad.

"What do you mean, *not really?*" Most of the time, she knew Jonathon's schedule better than her own. If he'd been within fifty miles of Palo Verde in the last five years, she would have known about it.

"I mean, sure, he never visits." Lacey spoke around a mouthful of waffle. "But it's not like we don't all know he's out there. Keeping an eye on us."

"Keeping an *eye* on you?" Wendy asked.

"Sure. Just watching out for us, you know?"

No. Wendy didn't know. She didn't have the faintest clue what Lacey was talking about. Luckily Lacey was a babbler and kept talking.

"Just little stuff mostly." She rolled her shoulder in a shrug. "Though sometimes it was big stuff. It used to make Mom so mad."

"What kind of stuff?"

"Like, oh, I don't know. I guess it started with the lab at school."

"Uh-huh," Wendy said encouragingly.

"That was about ten years ago. I won the regional science fair, but we didn't have the cash for me to go to the state competition. The newspaper ran this article about a fundraiser we were doing at school to raise money for it. Then—bam—anonymous donor steps in to cover the costs. The next year, the school district science labs were completely remodeled—middle school, all the way up to high school."

Lacey forked off another bite of her waffle, while Wendy poked listlessly at hers.

"I used to think that we were just incredibly, unbelievably lucky."

"What do you mean?"

"Well, like the science lab. I needed money and it magically appears. Or the time when Mom was out of work—this was before she got married—and this frozen-food delivery truck broke down right outside our house. The driver begged us to take the food inside to our own freezer before it went bad. Stuff like that happened all the time."

"And you think Jonathon was responsible?"

"Well, sure. Who else could it be? It's always made

Mom so mad, but I kind of like it. It's nice knowing he's out there, keeping an eye out for us."

"Why does it make your Mom mad?"

"Because she always says it'd be nicer to have her brother back."

It was so like him. He wanted to help. Always wanted to be the hero, but never wanted the credit for it. He never wanted to be beholden to anyone. Never wanted to risk having someone know he was a decent guy beneath the mantle of corporate greed he wore. And he never let anyone close enough to see the man he really was underneath.

No wonder it pissed off Marie. Hell, it pissed her off.

"He finally wore Mom down," Lacey was saying. "I think it was the scholarship that did it."

"There's a scholarship?" Wendy asked, then instantly realized how stupid that sounded. With Jonathon's fervor for education, *of course* there would be scholarship.

Lacey nodded. "Ten top science students in the high school get a full ride to the university of their choice as long as they major in a science or engineering program."

"Naturally."

How had she not known about any of this?

She had thought she had her thumb in every pie on his plate, but here was this one element of his life that she'd never glimpsed until now.

He'd told her he'd cut himself off from his family entirely. Claimed that he had nothing to do with them anymore. And yet now she found out he'd been meddling in their lives for years. Not bad meddling, just…from a distance.

Which was the way he did everything. God forbid he let anyone get truly close.

"Hey. Yoowoo?"

Wendy looked up to see Lacey waving her fork back and forth in front of Wendy's face. Apparently she'd been caught drifting off into what-the-hell-have-I-got-myself-into land. "Oh. Sorry. I was just lost in thought."

Lacey smirked. "Obviously. No one lets waffles this good go uneaten without good reason."

Well, at least confidence ran in the family.

"I was just…wondering what to think about all this."

"All what?"

"The generosity. The altruism."

"Really?" Lacey's expression turned shrewd and assessing. "Because if I was with a guy like that, it would be one of the things I loved most about him."

"Well, sure. It would have been. If I'd known about it." She gave her waffle a particularly savage poke.

"Oh, no." Lacey had gone pale. "I've made you doubt him."

"Lacey—"

"This is my fault." She shoved back her chair, stood up and waggled her hands frantically. "He's finally met someone he can be happy with, and I have to go and screw it up."

"This isn't your fault." Wendy jumped to her feet and grabbed Lacey's hands before she could knock herself out with one of them. "If this is anyone's fault, it's his. He's the one who's emotionally unavailable."

"No!" Lacey interrupted. "He's totally available! I promise! He's just…shy!"

Wendy paused, staring at Lacey with raised eyebrows. "Shy? You think Jonathon is *shy?*"

"Okay," Lacey admitted. "Not shy. He just doesn't talk about his feelings much."

"Or at all."

"But I know he has them. I know he does. He just doesn't talk about them. I mean, not to you. But he does to Peyton," Lacey blurted out, trying to be helpful.

And here she'd thought her eyebrows couldn't go

any higher. "He talks to Peyton? About his feelings?"

Sure, he was good with Peyton. Great with her as a matter of fact, but Wendy couldn't actually imagine him pouring his heart out to her.

"Yes, he does!" Lacey's words flew out in a garbled rush. "Last night, I woke up around one and I went to the kitchen for a glass of water, but before I got there, I heard him talking to Peyton. He was holding her on his lap and giving her a bottle and he told her that she was worth more to him than a hundred peppermint Pop Rocks."

Lacey stopped, her eyes wide and hopeful. As if what she'd said was supposed to convince Wendy. Or make sense.

"Um…it is possible you were dreaming?"

"No. This definitely happened."

"Jonathon told Peyton she was worth more to him than *peppermint Pop Rocks?*"

Lacey frowned. "I guess that's strange, huh?"

"A little." She didn't think they even made peppermint Pop Rocks.

"Okay, maybe I heard wrong. I didn't want to interrupt, so I snuck back to bed."

Wendy dropped Lacey's hands, her mind suddenly whirling. "Peppermint Pop Rocks" made no sense.

But “government contracts” did. That sounded more like it.

Wendy fished her phone out of her back pocket and pulled up her mother’s number. After a few seconds of ringing, her mother answered. “Hey, Mom, are you at breakfast yet?” She rolled her eyes as her mother answered. “Yes, I know it’s early. I need to talk to Uncle Hank. Put him on. Right now.”

Eighteen

She ended the call after only a few minutes. It didn't take long for her to verify what she already suspected. Then she made a beeline for the guest bedroom where they'd slept last night, dodging two kids jumping gleefully on a blow-up bed in the living room. Neither Jonathon nor Peyton were in the guest bedroom. But the door to the master bedroom was open, and when she glanced inside, she saw Peyton gurgling happily on the bed as Natalie, one of Jonathon's teenage nieces, dangled a toy over her.

"Honey," she asked, struggling to keep the simmering anger out of her voice. "Do you know where Jonathon is?" It was a struggle to keep her voice light.

The teenager looked up. “He asked me to watch Peyton while he took a shower.”

“Thanks.”

Wendy spun on her heel and stalked out into the hall to the bathroom. She gave the door a tap, and waited only until she heard him say, “Just a minute.” She slipped through the door without waiting for an invitation.

“What the—”

“We need to talk.”

She shut the door behind her, looking up just in time to see him grabbing a towel to cover himself. Behind him the shower was already on, pumping steam out into the room. Despite her anger, she felt her gaze clinging to the sight of his naked chest. Logically, after a week of sleeping in the same room with him, she should have started developing a Jonathon immunity. But instead, the sight of him affected her even more strongly. All that bare skin. Lightly tanned. The muscles that were defined, but not pronounced. The towel slung low across his waist as he tucked it in. It was all very, very…she drew in a slow breath…just very masculine. And distracting.

She forced her gaze up to his eyes, only to find him grinning at her. As if he could read every salacious thought in her head.

"Do you need something?" he asked in a low voice.

His arrogance brought her anger back to her in full force.

Yeah. She needed something. She needed to take his ego down a couple of notches. And then she needed some answers.

"Did my uncle try to blackmail you?"

Every muscle in Jonathon's body tensed. At least, every muscle she could see. Which was a lot of them.

Despite that, he kept his expression carefully schooled. If he hadn't been nearly naked, she might not have realized how strong his reaction was.

"Who have you been talking to?" he asked.

"Just answer my question."

He opened his mouth, clearly debating what to say.

Then there was a knock on the door.

"Give me a minute," he snapped, and she wasn't sure if he was speaking to her or to the person knocking.

"I have to go pee-pee and someone's in the other bathroom," came a small voice from the other side of the door.

Jonathon glared at her as if this was her fault.

She shrugged and mouthed the name "Sara."

Jonathon nodded her to the door in a get-out gesture.

Wendy shook her head.

"I need to go really, really bad!"

Little wonder since just a few minutes ago she'd seen the girl jumping on the bed.

"I don't think I can hold it!"

They could hear the thump-thump-thump of the girl bouncing up and down.

Wendy toed off her shoes and socks and kicked them near the wastepaper basket. Jonathon arched an eyebrow in question, but she ignored him as she pulled back the shower curtain and stepped into the steaming shower. The last thing she saw before she pulled the curtain closed was the expression of pure exasperation on his face. As if this was all terribly beneath him.

"Come on in," she heard him say. "But be fast."

"Ugh. Uncle Jonny, you're naked!" she heard the girl say.

"I was about to get in the shower," he said, his tone far dryer than Wendy now was. Even pressing herself toward the back wall, the spray kicked up onto the legs of her jeans.

"Aren't you going to go?" she heard Jonathon ask.

"Not while you're watching!" the girl whined.

"I'll turn around." Wendy heard the impatience in Jonathon's voice.

"Just get in the shower. And don't listen!" There was a moment of silence, during which Wendy imagined Jonathon mustering his patience. "Go!"

She saw Jonathon's fingers wrap around the edge of the shower curtain. She stepped under the showerhead to make room for him. An instant later, he pulled back the curtain and stepped in, towel still slung low across his hips.

The water slashed down, wetting her hair and clothes. She was drenched within moments. Jonathon raked his gaze over her, his expression dark. She felt his stare like a touch, searingly hot and disconcerting. A shiver ran down her spine and she tried to tell herself that her damp clothes had made her cold, but she knew that was a lie. She wasn't cold at all. How could she be when Jonathon was so close? And nearly naked? He looked her up and down, making her painfully aware of her clothes clinging to her skin and of her nipples hardened against the silk of her bra. Desire mingled with her anger in a potent mix that made her head spin.

From the other side of the curtain, she could hear Sara moving in the bathroom. Then the girl started singing "The Ants Go Marching." Jonathon arched an eyebrow at Wendy and suddenly the mood shifted, and she barely suppressed a giggle. The toilet flushed. The water ran colder for a few seconds, making Wendy shiver for real. Then the sink ran. A moment later the bathroom door opened and closed.

Suddenly, they were alone. In the shower. She was drenched and he was nearly naked.

This seemed like a very bad idea.

"Now," he said, his tone tight and controlled, "will you please get out of the bathroom? Let me finish my shower. In peace."

"No." The word left her mouth before she could even fully process his request. But the instant she said it, she knew it was the right response. "I'm not leaving. Not until you answer me. Did my uncle blackmail you into getting an annulment?"

"No. Now get out."

"But—"

"Get out. Now. Or I can't be responsible for my actions."

"I'm not leaving until you explain—"

He didn't even give her a chance to finish her sentence, but pulled her to him and crushed her mouth with a kiss.

Her hands shoved uselessly at his shoulders even

as her hips bumped eagerly against his. Her mouth opened under his assault, her tongue stroking his, savoring the taste of his hunger. Of his impatience. Every instinct she had screamed at her, but she could hardly distinguish her warring desires. She wanted him. She didn't want to want him. Her body desired him, but every shred of common sense she had warned her to stay away. He could bring her body enormous pleasure, but he'd surely crush her heart.

But when he touched her like this, she simply didn't care.

His kiss was deep and needy, as if he were trying to consume her. His hands seemed to be everywhere at once, meddling with the water coursing over her body in a chorus of stimulation. He touched her hair, her neck, her breasts. Teased the sensitive skin of her waist and massaged her nipples through her bra. Then under her bra. He peeled off her shirt and bra and they fell to the floor of the shower in a sodden lump. Then he was caressing her again. It was as if he was trying to absorb her very essence through his hands. As if he was binding her to him.

Or maybe that was just her, projecting her own emotions onto him. Because she couldn't stop touching him. Couldn't keep her hands from exploring all that glorious naked skin. Her fingers trembled with need as she reached for the towel. But stopped herself just in time. Instead, she flattened her palm against his chest and pushed.

"Stop," she said.

He stilled instantly, pulling back from her. She sank against the wall of the shower, her breath coming in ragged breaths.

This was the problem with their relationship. Physically, they were a perfect match. And if that was enough for her, then…this would be enough for her.

If all she wanted was fantastic sex, then it wouldn't matter to her that Jonathon had prevaricated about her uncle. If all she wanted was a husband to satisfy her family, then Jonathon would still be the perfect man. But she wanted more than that now. She wanted all of him.

Shaken to her very core, she reached over and turned off the water. She yanked back the curtain and grabbed a towel off the rack. Giving her hair a quick rub, she climbed out of the shower.

She looked over her shoulder and saw that he'd turned his back to her. He stood with his arm braced against the wall, resting his head on his forearm. As if he was struggled for control. Yeah, well, she felt the same.

"Why'd you lie?" she asked.

He looked up, turning around. "What?"

It was an effort for her to keep from looking down, but she managed it. "About my uncle. Why'd you lie about him blackmailing you?"

"I didn't." He grabbed a towel as well and scrubbed it down his face.

"I talked to my uncle. I know the truth."

For an instant, surprise flickered across his face, but he hid it well. "Then you know that he didn't blackmail me. He made the offer. I refused. That's not blackmail. That's attempted blackmail."

She stared at him blankly and after a moment all she could do was let out a bark of laughter. "That is just like you to try to get off on a technicality."

"You're mad at me about this?" The confusion in his voice was real. "What good would it do you to know that your uncle is a jackass?"

"I already knew that." She fished her shirt off the floor of the tub and gave it a vicious twist to wring out the water. "What good does it do you to try to hide it from me?"

"I was just—"

"Trying to protect me?" she finished for him as she pulled the shirt over her head. "Yeah. I get that. But you've got to stop doing me favors. Because it's not helping things at all."

"I don't know what you mean."

"Of course you don't." She gave a sharp, bitter laugh. She shook her head. He may be brilliant when it came to money, but when it came to emotions, he was an idiot. "I now know why you've been so determined to make this work. I just don't think you understand it yet."

"What are you even talking about?"

"You walked away from your family when you were so young and you still haven't found a way back to them. And you haven't made peace with that either."

"What does my family have to do with any of this?"

"You love kids. You'd be a great dad, but you don't feel worthy of having a family of your own. Not when you walked away from your family. So Peyton and I, we're consolation prizes. You get to have a family, but you get to lie to yourself and pretend you're doing it for FMJ or to protect me."

"You're wrong."

"I don't think I am. You're just so out of touch with what you really want, that you don't even recognize what's going on. Think about it, why did you marry me in the first place?"

"So you could keep custody of Peyton."

"No, that's why I married you. Not why you married me. You asked me to marry you, because it was supposed to be best for FMJ. I was going to leave and you were trying to protect the company. But somewhere along the way, you lost track of that. The company is supposed to come first for you."

His jaw tightened and his gaze drew dark. "It's not supposed to come before my wife."

"No. I'm your assistant. Before I was your wife, I was just the incredibly efficient, supremely organized, very best assistant you've ever had. That's why you married me. Because it was best for FMJ." She cupped his jaw in her hand and gently tilted his face down so he met her gaze. "I'm going to make this easy for you. Your loyalties lie with FMJ. With Ford and Matt. That's where they've always been. That's okay."

"Stop it!" He barked the order, jerking away from her hand. "It's not your decision to make."

She felt her lips curving in a bittersweet smile. "You really think it matters to my uncle which of us capitulates? Hell, he'll probably be glad it was me who broke."

"Is that what you're doing? You're giving in to your uncle?" There was a sneer of scorn in his voice, but she knew the pain it hid.

"If I accept my uncle's bargain for you, you get that government contract. FMJ wins."

She kept her voice calm and reasonable, even though her emotions were tearing her apart.

"I am not—" he growled "—going to sacrifice our marriage just so FMJ can win some stupid government contract."

"No. But I'm going to. You're not the only one who loves this company. I believe in it. And I believe you're going to continue to do great things with it, even if I'm not there. So don't disappointment me, okay?"

"That's it?" Jonathon asked, outrage pouring through him. "You're just going to walk away?"

"It's what I should have done to begin with."

"No. I don't believe that. I don't believe *you* believe that." She didn't even look at him as she straightened her sopping-wet shirt. Didn't even meet his gaze. And for the first time since this ridiculous conversation started, he considered the possibility that she was actually going to do it. That she was really going to walk out the door and leave him.

He grabbed her by the arm and turned her to face him. "If you really want to leave me, then fine. I can live with that. But don't lie to me and tell me you're doing it because it's what's best for FMJ. Don't lie to yourself either."

"Okay, you want the truth? Here it is—I know how important this deal is to you and I can't let you throw it away. Not for me. If I did, you'd only end up resenting me someday. And I couldn't stand that."

Then he said the one thing he thought might make a difference. "Don't forget, we've slept together. That annulment won't be so easy to get now. And I'm not going to make it easy for you to walk away from me."

She looked at him, meeting his gaze directly. There was something so sad in her eyes that his heart actually contracted a bit as she looked at him. Her lips curved into a smile that held no humor, but brimmed with warmth and sorrow. "It was never going to be easy to walk away from you. I knew that all along."

And with that, she left the room, her clothes dripping water in her wake. For what must have been a full minute, he stared after her, shocked that she'd actually done it, even though she'd said she would.

Then he slung a dry towel around his waist and ran after her, following the drops of water like a little trail of breadcrumbs. He dashed through the family room, barely aware of the curious gazes that followed his half-naked progress through the house. Then he stopped and ran back to the guest room where he and Wendy had slept the previous night. Natalie sat alone on the bed, looking confused.

"Did she take Peyton?" he demanded.

"Yeah." Natalie gave a confused shrug. "She ran in here, grabbed the baby and the suitcase and ran out. Where is she—"

He didn't wait to hear the rest of her question, but dashed back through the house. He heard adult laughter and one of his nieces ask, "Mommy, why is he naked?"

He made it out onto the front lawn in time to see Wendy close the backseat door and then climb into the driver's seat. The towel slipped as he ran for the car. Holding the drooping ends of the towel in one hand, he banged on the window with the other. But she didn't stop or even slow down. And a second later, he was left standing on the street. In a towel.

And since she'd taken his car, he had no way to get home.

Scratch that. Since she'd left and was taking Peyton with her, he no longer had a home.

Nineteen

Jonathon stood there in the road for a long time, watching the corner around which his Lexus had just disappeared.

He might have stood there all day, shock pinning him to the ground, if his sister hadn't walked out in the street to stand beside him. Arms crossed over her chest, she looked him up and down. "Wow, you really effed that up, didn't you?"

He shot her a look of annoyance. "After all these years, how is it that you're still this irritating?"

She grinned. "I'm a big sister. It's our moral obligation to point it out when you make a colossal mistake."

"Thanks," he muttered dryly. "Very helpful."

Glancing back at the house, he realized that Marie's brood—all five kids, plus the husband—had poured out onto the lawn after them. In fact, they'd even attracted the attention of a few neighbors. Little wonder. How often did you see a guy in nothing but a towel running after a car?

He turned around and headed back to the house. Marie fell into step beside him. "What are you going to do?"

"What do you think I'm going to do?"

Marie smiled. "The brother I remember would chase her down and win her back."

He nodded, hoping he looked more confident than he felt. "I'm going to need to borrow your car."

"Borrow?" Lacey laughed. "No way. You think we're going to let you do this all on your own?"

"I did hope," he admitted in exasperation. But when had his family ever done what he wanted them to do?

"Too bad," Mark said. "This is the most entertaining thing that's happened since that toy company's truck crashed on our corner and all the kids on the block got free toys the week before Christmas."

Wendy briefly considered skipping the hotel and driving straight back to her apartment in Palo

Alto. After confronting Jonathon, the last thing she wanted was to see her own family. However she still needed to convince Mema she was the best mother for Peyton and abandoning them without a word in Palo Verde would do little to help her cause. And since she wasn't going to have that rich husband in her favor anymore, she figured she needed all the help she could get.

Besides, she had unfinished business with her uncle.

The historic Ellington House hotel sat in the middle of town, on Main Street, a block or two from Cutie Pies. She nabbed one of the parking spots on the street. She dug around in the suitcase and pulled out a dry shirt and jeans. It was tricky changing in the car without drawing attention to herself, but she managed it. Plus it gave her time to muster her courage, before she extracted Peyton from the car seat and headed into the hotel.

When she'd called her mom earlier, her entire family had just met for breakfast on the terrace of the hotel's dining room. If she was lucky, they'd be just finishing up and she could get this all over at once.

Striding with purpose, she carried Peyton through the lobby and up the stairs to the second-story dining room. On another day, the hotel's elegance and meticulous restoration might have impressed her. As it was, she barely noticed the velvet-trimmed antiques and heavy oak furnishings.

Instead, she made a beeline for the double doors leading onto the patio. That was where she found them, sitting at a long table overlooking Main Street. Mema was at one end, Uncle Hank at the other. Her parents, Hank Jr. and Helen scattered in between. They all looked at ease among the fine china and sterling teapots, the poached eggs and hollandaise sauces. The meal was so perfectly her family.

No homemade banana chocolate-chip waffles here. Just elegant dining and a steely determination to ignore the tension simmering beneath the surface. This would be her life from now on.

She dreaded this with every fiber of her being. Yet it was still preferable to the life she was walking away from. She knew how important FMJ was to Jonathon. Its success had always been his first priority. She couldn't knowingly ruin all he'd planned for the company.

If she did, she'd be stuck on the sidelines in her own family, Jonathon's heart forever just out of her reach.

She stopped at Mema's end of the table. Peyton

still propped on her hip, Wendy said, to the table in general, "Okay. You win."

Uncle Hank's face split in a wide grin. Helen's eyes lit up as if someone had just offered to sprinkle full-carat diamonds on her plate as a garnish. Hank Jr. just looked bored, as he had ever since setting foot in California.

Her mother and father exchanged worried looks. Looks that seemed—for once—to reveal actual concern for her. Maybe there would be an upside to this debacle after all. Her heart would be broken into a thousand pieces, but maybe the pieces her parents had broken years ago would start to heal. It gave her hope that maybe the parts Jonathon had broken would someday heal as well.

Mema dabbed at her mouth with her napkin, then nodded to a spare chair at another table. "Well, Gwen, since you've interrupted our meal yet again, you might as well pull up a chair and explain yourself." Then she shot an annoyed look at Helen. "Helen, dear, please try to contain your glee."

Somehow despite the situation, Wendy felt herself smiling. Funny how her overbearing family wasn't quite so unbearable now that she was an adult in her own right. Now that she was coming to them on her own terms.

Her father jumped up to pull a chair over for her and Wendy seated herself between her mother and her grandmother. Surveying the table, she felt oddly at peace about her decision. Yes, this would be her life from now on. Sometimes.

She would inevitably have to deal with them and so would Peyton. But this wouldn't have to be their only life. The two of them, together, could find their own way as a family. They could endure hollandaise sauce every once in a while, as long as they had banana chocolate-chip waffles most of the time.

Pinning her uncle with her gaze, she started with, "I fully expect you to honor the deal you offered Jonathon."

His grin widened only slightly. "Why, certainly."

Then she turned to her parents. "Mama, Daddy," she began. "I'd like to finally accept—"

But before she could tell them she'd like to take the job at Morgan Oil, the door to the terrace swung open behind her. Mentally cursing the wait staff for interrupting her big moment of capitulation, she turned in her seat to send them away.

Only it wasn't some overeager busboy. It was Jonathon. Along with what—at first glance—appeared to be every Bagdon in the county.

She jolted to her feet. "What the—"

"I'm not letting you go," he said unceremoniously.

For the first time since she'd known him, Jonathon looked decidedly disheveled, if that was possible for a man who kept his hair trimmed into such neat submission. He was dressed in jeans and a rumpled denim work shirt open over—bizarrely enough—a T-shirt, for some rap group, which was obviously too tight.

Clutching Peyton tighter to her chest, she tried her damnedest to glare him down. "I'm not having this discussion here."

"Then you shouldn't have rushed off." He quirked his eyebrow. "If you want, we can drive back over to my sister's and finish the conversation in the shower."

Helen gave an indignant huff, but beside her Hank Jr. sniggered. Then there was the unmistakable whack of someone getting kicked under the table followed by his grunt of pain. Wendy glanced over her shoulder to see Mema smiling faintly.

"My dear, since there is now no hope of us finishing our breakfast in peace, you should at least hear him out."

"Okay." She eyed him suspiciously. "Start talking."

But before he could say a word, Lacey darted between them and held out her hands. "Let me take Peyton. I have the feeling you're going to want your arms free before this is over."

"She's fine here," Wendy said stubbornly.

"Oh, for goodness' sake, Wendy," muttered her mother, standing. "If anyone is going to take Peyton, it should be me." Her mother practically wrestled the baby out of Wendy's arms.

With nothing to hold, Wendy wrapped her arms around her chest. "Go ahead," she said to Jonathon.

He opened his mouth, then snapped it shut again, casting a wary glance at the crowd around them, her family on one side, his family blocking the only door back into the hotel. He grabbed her arm and navigated her around the few empty tables to the far corner of the terrace.

"I want another chance to make this work. You and I are good together."

"Good together in bed?" she asked softly. "I'm not going to argue that. Good together at work? Absolutely. But I want more than that." She swallowed. "I need more than that."

Jonathon scrapped a hand over his short hair, his mouth pressed into a straight line as he seemed to be mustering his words. He studied her face, looking for what, she wasn't sure.

Refusing to meet his gaze, her eyes dropped again to the absurd T-shirt. Frustrated that he claimed to want to talk, but still wasn't talking, she asked, "And why on earth are you wearing that T-shirt?"

"That's mine!" called a voice from near the door, shattering the illusion of privacy.

She looked around Jonathon's shoulder to see Lacey's younger brother Thomas holding up a hand.

Jonathon rolled his eyes in obvious exasperation. "You took our suitcase. I didn't have any clothes other than the jeans."

"Oh." She cringed. "Sorry. I didn't mean to leave you with nothing—"

"Then don't leave me with nothing," he interjected. "Don't you get it? If you leave at all, you leave me with nothing."

The tightness in her chest loosened a little. "Go on," she prodded.

"I don't know, maybe your wacky theory about me leaving my family is right. Maybe I have never forgiven myself for walking away from my family. And maybe that's why I haven't married before now. But that's not why I married you."

She finally let herself meet his gaze. The naked emotion she saw there stripped her breath away. But just seeing it wasn't enough. She needed to hear it.

She needed him to say it aloud. "Okay, then. Why did you marry me?"

"Why do you think I married you?" he countered.

"If it was enough for me to just intuit how you feel about me, then we wouldn't have a problem. But it's not enough. I need to hear the words. From you. I need you to say it aloud." Frustrated, she reached up and cupped his jaw in her hands, forcing him to look her in the eyes. "Whatever you feel, it isn't going to scare me off."

"I love you, Wendy. I think I've always loved you." His lips curved into a smile. "That may not scare you, but it scares the crap out of me. Because I don't know what I'd do if you left me."

She bit down on her lip, trying to hold back the tears of joy threatening to spill over. "Better," she said finally. "Go on," she coaxed.

"Okay." He blew out a rough breath. "The way I see it, you can't leave me without voiding the terms of the prenup."

Her eyebrows shot up. "Huh?"

"You were the one who said that when the marriage ends, we each walk away with everything we had when we started. But if you left now, you'd walk away with my heart."

Someone behind them groaned. Then Thomas

called out, "Dude, I hope that sounded cooler in your head. 'Cause that was lame."

Jonathon's eyes drifted closed for an instant and he gave a nod of chagrin. "It actually did sound cooler in my head."

"I thought it sounded great!" Lacey called out.

Wendy threaded her fingers through Jonathon's hair and pulled his mouth down to hers. Just before his lips touched hers, she admitted, "I thought it sounded pretty good too."

His mouth was warm and moist over hers. The kiss sweet and gentle. Full of love. Full of potential.

When he lifted his head, she said, "I love you, Jonathon Bagdon. If this scares you, then you're not alone. Because it terrifies me too. Everything about it. But I figured, at least we're not alone in it."

He flashed her one of those rare smiles that squeezed her heart and didn't let go. "I love you, Gwendolyn Leland Morgan Bagdon. Will you marry me?" Then he grinned and added, "Again."

She flung her arms around him and whispered a yes into his ear. Then added, "You know I prefer just the simple Wendy Bagdon."

She glanced around Jonathon's shoulder to see Lacey giving her a big thumbs-up. Thomas was still shaking his head, as though the uncle he barely knew had been a huge disappointment. Marie had leaned her back against her husband's chest and he'd wrapped an arm around her. They were both grinning widely.

Wendy's own family looked less exuberant. Uncle Hank was scowling. Hank Jr. had pulled out his BlackBerry and was checking his messages. Helen had her arms crossed over her chest, looking about ten seconds away from a meltdown. But her mother was smiling and as Wendy watched, her father gave her mother's hand a squeeze. Even Mema seemed—almost—to be smiling.

Wendy nodded in her uncle's direction and whispered to Jonathon. "What about the government contract?"

He scoffed. "Who cares? One decision isn't going to change the course of FMJ's future. One government contract won or lost isn't going to make or break the company."

"It's a lot of money."

"And we're a diverse company. We'll be fine."

"You're sure?" she asked, because she hated to think he might regret the decision down the road.

By way of answering, he grabbed her hand and pulled her back over to the table where her family still sat.

He draped an arm over her shoulder and pulled her against his chest. "Henry," he began formally. "If you'd like, we can negotiate visitation rights for you, but only if you back off." He shifted his gaze to Helen. "If anyone in this family wants to fight for Peyton, then bring it on. Just know that we're going to fight for her. We have every intention of winning. No matter how much it costs. And if you do bring this fight to our doorstep, when you lose, you won't ever see Peyton or Wendy again."

Before Uncle Hank could say anything, Mema pushed back her chair and stood slowly. "I don't think we need to worry about that. Though I do expect to see both my granddaughter and my great-granddaughter more often now that she's settled down."

"We can do that." Jonathon nodded formally. Then he gave Wendy's shoulder a squeeze. "Now, if you'll excuse us, I'm going to take my bride and my daughter and we're going to go have breakfast." He glanced down at her. "How does a doughnut from Cutie Pies sound?"

"Perfect."

She didn't mention the banana chocolate-chip waffles. That seemed like a lifetime ago anyway.

They walked the few blocks to Cutie Pies with

Jonathon's family trailing behind. They'd almost reached the restaurant, when Wendy asked, "When did you realize you loved me?"

He stopped walking and looked down at her. "I think I've always loved you." Then he laughed. "You didn't really think I asked you to marry me just to keep you from quitting, did you?"

"Yeah," she admitted. "I did."

"Come on, nobody's that good of an assistant."

She socked him in the arm. "Excuse me, but yes I am!"

"You are an amazing assistant." He dropped a kiss onto her forehead. "But you're an even better wife."

* * * * *